Printed in the United Kingdom

First Printing, January 2018

ISBN 9781977025258

Dedicated to Matthew

Heartmender

A novel by Bradley Axe

Scenes

Alex wiped her brow as she sat anxiously in the humid night. Even though it was nearing midnight it was still warm enough to justify fanning herself with her own hand in a futile attempt to stay cool.

No, he don't like that, too ambient to be descriptive, too descriptive to be ambient.

He backed up and tried again.

Alex brushed her hair away from her face as she sat, still, in the lingering summer air; breathing was raspy and uneven as she sat under the thick orange glow of streetlights, perched on the garden wall waiting for the reason of her waiting to show their face.

No, who writes like this? That's probably not the correct use of a semicolon either. This is worse than the original.

He backed up and tried again.

The air was still, thick, humid, Alex wiped her brow and looked around, trying to do anything to take her mind off of the heat. The amber glow of the streetlight...

No, too specific a colour.

...the orange glow of the streetlight served only to pierce the still Vermont night with warm colour.

How was this all he'd gotten after half an hour? It all seemed so natural an hour ago when the night was so vivid and crisp he could taste the musty air and could feel Alex's sweat on his own face. He'd even figured out the first line of conversation, the character establishing conversation between Alex and Harry that would spark the camaraderie, now all locked from the paper by his own pen.

Mark got up and left his desk, sliding the failed papers into the wastebasket on the way out. He wrangled up whatever he could get to make himself presentable for the night and took a deep breath. Another story idea lost to the aether thanks to his inability to be the right person to tell it. He thought of Alex, Harry, Vic, and Hector while he changed into more presentable clothes, unable to let the image of the four of them on that park bench in America go. He contrasted the image of them melting in their shirts in the mid-summer heat with him disinterestedly looking at the will-they-won't-they autumnal rain clouds looming over the Midlands. He debated calling up the party and feigning illness so he wouldn't have to walk but knew he, frustratingly, did *want* to be there.

After a tricky descent involving at least two kicked boxes thanks to a poorly placed lightswitch, he opened up the basement spirit cabinet and pulled out a Vodka bottle. It was nothing fancy but money's tight and he figured Polly was a good enough sport to at least share some if he'd made it sound like he'd put in a lot of effort to buy it for her. After pulling out a cheap rum for himself and closing the cabinet he took a look around, one of the things he'd kicked had landed in a pile of old newspapers that desperately needed sorting into "not containing my work" and "containing my work: burn". The other had ricocheted into a string of pipes and somehow done a hefty dent on one. He leant over and took a big whiff, nothing was leaking, not time to call in the landlord just yet.

Mark made his way back up and slipped out the front door. The rain must've already come and gone while working, he thought, immediately stepping around and over the puddles on the sidewalk. He locked his front door and made a concerted effort to leave the Vermont troublemakers inside, but Alex stayed on his mind as he began to walk away, she'd captured his attention and nested in his mind as he meandered his way to Polly's.

Polly's party was a slick little do in her back garden, Mark tried to knock the front door but the lump in his throat at what to say when Polly answered gave him time to overhear the garden and walk around instead. He was one of the first few people there and he cautiously looked around. No sight of Polly, there was a Jason, a Kelly ,and a Don, but no Polly. Mark let out a sigh of relief and sat under the awning, exchanging polite acknowledgement nods to Kelly and Don who were already deep in their own conversation. Sitting down next to Jason was an intentional move, easy to talk too and a purveyor of comfortable silences Jason was the best party guest one could meet.

Mark held out a hand to be shaken and let it hang until Jason had noticed.

Trying to stick on his please-be-gentle voice, Mark began. "Evening Jason". He looked and immediately saw the smile of a gentle giant come across Jason's face.

"Slimey!" Jason beamed "Nice to see you made it, thought you'd bail on us"

"Please, acting like you're not the accomplice to that nickname" Mark quipped back placing his bottles on the table, intentionally trying to cover the own-brand Rum behind the Vodka from Jason's perspective "Besides, needed to get out, work was depressing me"

Jason pressed the back of his hand to his forehead and feigned a fever "Oh heaven forbid those local pastry eating contests and dog-poo-bag controversies be late to the Press's doorstep. Surely that would result in the collapse of old media as we know it!" He threatened to fall back in his chair as his actions became more and more exaggerated "I can only hope the valuable time you have freed to visit us can be recovered swiftly!"

They both had a laugh and Jason took a swig of his beer, and brew with a logo in a language unknown to him.

After looking around Mark asked "So where is the birthday girl anyway?"

"Gone to pick up some friends, work ones I think." Jason, somehow managing to put emphasis on every word, responded.

Mark let out a comically understated sigh and took a lick of the Rum. Looking up at the clouds parting, he let his mind drift onto Polly, Jason, and himself; he'd began to forget about Alex by then.

He must've let himself zone out fully because next thing he knew he was being entombed by a sleek pair of arms in a welcoming embrace. Polly was back.

"Polly!"

"Marky!"

"Polly..."

"Marky!"

"Can you please reposition yourself so returning this hug is not overly difficult?"

"Oh, sorry"

She moved over and sat between him and Don, she hugged again, this time in a repricatable way and picked up the Vodka

Mark tried to keep pace "Oh yeah, that's for you, it's special stuff!"

"Cheeky", she smiled and opened the lid, "Well played Marky, I'll give this a whirl sometime tonight" She gave a big smile, not the same as Jason's, Polly's was much more of a suppressed, tasteful giggle of a smile than the hearty belly laugh of Jason's. She radiated the kind of inexplicable sunlight from every movement and Mark was always enthralled to simply watch her subtleties.

She was gorgeous. Tonight was the right time.

The rest of the night went along smoothly. Mark floated around the party for most of the night. He tried to stay stuck near Polly, Jason and occasionally to one of the handful of mutuals he vaguely knew. Polly had good taste in friends and everyone there was generally pleasant to speak to, with plenty of "oh so you know..."s and "yes I remember you there..."s. All surrounded by a pleasant atmosphere in the garden and later, after the rain came, in the living room that demonstrated Polly's warmth extended to her home as well. The night went on, more rum was consumed until the confidence that it provided was in full effect, and Mark eventually seized his chance to say what he wanted to Polly. He could see she was saying goodbye to a few guests he didn't recognize and took the chance to start the next conversation. After sidled his way over to her he placed himself in a way where he could immediately grab her attention when she was done. Close enough where he could overhear the goodbyes and, though he was actively trying to not be rude, he couldn't help hearing what was loud and nearby.

"...it's been fun seeing you again Polly. You should get a train down to see me and the husband some time"

"Oh I certainly will Sydney!". Mark latched onto the oddness of the guest's name.

"Either way, I have to fly, you have to give me a message soon and let me know about Mark!" Mark pricked his ears up. His heart fluttered, a dozen and a half potential meanings to that spontaneous remark ran through his head, maybe she was planning something, maybe she secretly resented him and spent the whole night complaining, maybe she felt the same way. The feeling in his throat threatened to burst out in anticipation before they'd even finished speaking.

"I will do Sydney, I'm seeing him Sunday so I'll let you know after that! See you soon!" She closed the waved goodbye as he soaked in the information. Sunday? He knew nothing on plans on Sunday, maybe there was a surprise.

She turned around before he could finish thinking and was startled by his suddenly extremely zoned out look. "Marky! Didn't see you there!" she laughed and began scouring his facial expression "Are you pissed already?"

"Oh no no no no. I just..." split second thinking kicked in "...heard my name and thought you'd called me over"

She laughed again, she laughs a lot, it's a very nice laugh. "Sorry! I meant a Mark at work, not you. There's no way I'd talk like that behind your back and..." he zoned out immediately again, this time he had changed to a pensive sadness.

A different Mark, a different person, a date, a date with Mark, a date with a different Mark. The anchor in his throat sank all the way down to the pit of his stomach with a near-audible thunk. Polly stopped speaking, he didn't register the specific words but figured it was free to say anything.

"Sorry anyway Polly, I'd forgotten about how much work I have to get done so I need an early night. Anyway it's been great though, amazing seeing you again!" Mark had mustered up as cheery a voice as he could and gave a gentle hug before Polly could even register he was leaving. He walked out the door and began to walk home, in a stroke of luck it wasn't in the rain.

He'd already had the Rum bottle in his hands when he'd left so swigged it occasionally as he made his way back home. He felt sick. Sick that he'd let himself get so caught up in his own dreams. Sick that even after he'd figured it out and was walking away the brilliant light that she cast from her freckles to her nails never dimmed. Sick that he'd lost his chance. He felt sick that he felt sick, which made him feel more sick; because he was happy for her, he didn't even need to pretend he was. He knew a dear friend was about to find someone who she sees in him what he sees in her. He was sick that he was so jealous.

By the time he got to his front door his face was damp, gently wishing the rain had returned to make it less obvious, forgetting to lock the door behind him.

He sat down, pulled back out his notepad and a pen, and began writing about Alex. No, not Alex, he'd gotten numb to that name after so much thought. He was over Alex. He thought again of Polly. He wrote down Polly, scribbled it out, he was sober enough to have the intangible feeling that that was a bad idea. He wrote down the name Paula. The rest of his memory of the night was lost to his intense emotion and the near empty Rum that sat on his desk next to the pen pots.

II

Mark was awoken by a monster headache, the kind that signals a day spent moping around vainly attempting to reduce movements. Several attempts of rolling around eventually lead to him facing his alarm clock, 2 minutes from going off. Mark curled up and pressed the sheets against his head, trying to get a few more gentle moments of rest as well as hunkering down against the incoming cacophony signalling his time to get out. He filled the time turning over the events of the party in his head.

He wondered to himself why he'd left so early, regardless of the accidental bombshell that the existence of the other Mark was, he'd still been enjoying the himself and he was ultimately glad that Polly had found someone, his gut threatened to drop again as he thought about it though. He tried to remain in his head but couldn't deny that he was reacting to a hypothetical rejection with genuine despondence. He figured he should send Polly a real message: apologise for leaving so abruptly and maybe trying to encode it with an apology for acting like he was.

But after opening up his phone he found himself lingering on her profile, even in the still picture she lit up the room. A graceful boon of energy wormed into the atmosphere and seemed to make the natural beige and brown of his bedroom a veritable palette of gentle colours.

While lost in the eyes of Polly's profile picture of the Algarve, his alarm began, throwing off his grip and landing the corner of the phone directly between his eyes.

Sod that, he shut it off and dragged himself up, nearly falling over again due to a poor perception of the ground. He was still too tired and emotional to deal with whatever mess he'd left himself in last night. He wiped his nose, and spluttered himself a deep breath to place himself in the moment. Now was Coffee time. Later was emotional time.

His house was a mess, full of remnants of the rough night after he'd gotten back. As the Kettle whirred to life he clutched his eyebrows in deep thought. Trying to recall enough loose fragments of the night to at least fill in the gaps manually. But as the kettle clicked and he began to pour he'd always stop at the same place: at his desk about to start writing. The name Paula. Paula, Paula, Paula, that was the very last thing he remembered before waking up. The name orbited his head like a cuckoo. Why that name? Is it really just a choice based on the first letter P? Mark liked to think better of himself as a writer but remembered he once misspelled his name when reporting on a rural chicken competition so held his tongue.

Mark brought himself and his mug to his desk and fished through the tabletop. Many, many papers scattered in an order that made sense in an intoxicated state and to him now seemed like chaos. A page even used in an attempt to clean the now sideways bottle of rum's expelled contents yet still with a few inexplicable doodles of faces and spirals resembling flowers or hurricanes.

After fishing through the pages and sorting them in order. Mark sat back and looked out the window above the desk. Quashing his thoughts in the patter of the gentle rain threatening to get worse. He debated shredding the papers and getting back to work, but knew he was too tired to find a way to do it. He debated throwing them out in the trash, but what is the value of a writing if not to be read?

Mark sat down and read.

Knock Knock.

I cleared my throat and tried to peer through the window again, I could see directly into the kitchen and could see the lights were on but no immediate signs of any life. After a third knock on the window without response I took a step back and tried to peer into the first floor windows, every light was on but beyond that the front of the house gave away nothing.

A car pulled up behind me as I started contemplating turning back and double-checking the address. Turning around with the swift pivot of the heels I saw a wispy braid of blonde hair gesturing to a young couple linked in arms to follow. As we locked eyes both grew in excitement.

Mark stood up from his desk and looked out the window above his desk, he could've sworn as he read that line he heard a vehicle. Repositioning himself he could see the neighboring family of 3 getting out of their sedan. He let out a sigh of relief and returned his attention to the desk.

"Marky!" She exclaimed in a voice still as earnest and pure as the day we'd met. She extended her arms for a hug which I gladly accepted "So glad you came!".

"It's been a long time Paula" I laughed, trying to brush off my smitten face whilst presenting the present: an import Vodka straight from Poland "Last time we met was probably your last birthday!"

"Regardless, we should certainly fix that problem, now let's roll!"

She swapped from car to house keys and let me in, guiding me and the couple to the back garden where half a dozen guests had already congregated. I recognized a few from our days at University but there were a few complete unknowns whom she quickly introduced. Some old school friend, a few randoms and some work colleagues. I gave the standard suite of polite nods and the occasional handshake as I let their names in Paula's sweet melodious voice echo in my head. I always found it funny that hearing things in her voice made them easier to remember, her voice is just as enchanting as her it always seemed.

I was eventually left with the young couple she'd arrived with and began the small but ultimately satisfying banal chatter that one gets up to at parties. They were introduced as Alex and Ella, they seemed nice enough.

Mark nearly spat out his coffee in laughter has he read the names. He'd been impressed by how much he'd written but the contents kept wavering between a bit on the creepy side and the pathetically hilarious side. He thought to himself at the start of the night before sitting on how to introduce Alex to the page and how nonchalantly he'd dropped her in an unrelated work.

Alex talked a lot about how she'd moved over from America for a year of education and every word she spoke Ella hang onto them like her life depended on it.

Of course she had.

Whenever Ella got the chance to, or rather was made to, get a word in she kept immediately passing the conversation to someone else, trying desperately not to have the both of us linger on her at the same time. Except for one point after half an hour and a glass of wine when she started a topic.

"So Mark, how'd you know Paula?"

"Oh, we go back a few years, we met back at University down in Surrey. I was friends with her boyfriend at the time"

"Wait I thought she was single?" Alex interrupted.

"I thought she was gay" Ella glumly responded.

"Well they broke up a few years ago so keep your chin up and maybe you'll get a chance" I remarked, giving Ella a playful shove and noticing Alex's dagger-filled look out of the corner of my eyes "pretty sure she's been single ever since"

"She must be getting pretty old then" Alex slipped in, peering around me to get a look over my shoulder, probably where Paula was.

I laughed a little harder than I should've at how casually she slipped that one in and this time they both shot me a quizzical look. We'd only be about the same age give or take the year and their snide remark had inadvertently been a reminder of his own youth dwindling gently as the sunlight now slowly succumbing to the passive glimmer of moonlight.

"Low blow" Mark said aloud before catching himself. He and Polly were still in their twenties and he knew himself well enough that he'd certainly make himself younger on paper.

The night continued like that, I found home on a cushioned garden chair and found the best pastime between conversations and the occasional fit of dancing when shuffle pulled up something fitting was watching. Watching the various guests fading in and out of view as they grouped and regrouped, occasionally darting in the house and occasionally not returning. Sometimes others would join me but I let the night take its own course from there.

The night edged further to a close without much incident, at least no more incident that is typical when a group of millennial twenty-somethings get together. Stupid enough to drink themselves sick but smart enough to not do it anywhere hazardous. Mark crossed out hazardous and wrote problematic instead. By the time the sky ever so gently began to red there were only a small handful fighting the morning by holding onto the night.

I was in the middle of a surprisingly gripping discussion on the american civil war with a man whose name I never actually picked up when Polly and the final guest interrupted us.

"Taxi's here Chris"

Mark tried to remember if he knew a Chris. He pondered for a moment, certain he must have interacted with one at some point but not certain of where.

"Yeah alright, we're going down towards Mapleback, you near that Mark?"

I tried to hide my simultaneous relief that someone else had dropped his name in and embarrassment that he'd remembered mine as graciously as possible "Um... no, I'm other way; I'll walk it'll be ok".

Chris shrugged and gave his goodbyes, leaving me and Paula the last two in the garden.

We sat there for a long time, or at least for what felt like one, neither of us particularly interested in disturbing the quiet murmur of the suburban atmosphere. I listened to the taxi driving away from the house, the engine slowly getting quieter as it took the two elsewhere. I'd lied to Chris, I was good at it in small doses. Partly it was because I enjoyed a walk with myself to finish a night off, a physical and mental cool-down lap before I can fall into my bed and embrace the next day. But mostly it was because I knew that if I stayed, I'd be able to feel this exact moment. The two of us, Paula and I, us.

The twinkles of the stars eventually faded as we watched the sunrise, I felt myself nearly fall asleep as a side effect of the long night.

"Sorry, looks like I have to call it a night.

Polly stood up sharp, almost jolted by the reminder I was also there "Oh, of course, call it a morning more like".

I laughed and patted her on the shoulder "Yeah, more like".

A single beat of silence passed between us before I acted.

"I was wondering when we could see each other again, it totally sucks that it's only your birthdays."

"Yeah, I am sorry it's not more often, the right time doesn't come around often enough does it"

"I was thinking, how about we make time for it?

She tilted her head curiously.

"What I mean is, we don't have to wait for something to come around just to see each other. Maybe we can just do something together for the sake of doing it. Because you're really nice and I don't want to waste the chances to be around you more."

I mentally covered my mouth after saying that. Temporarily becoming incapable of thinking like the adults we were I'd resorted to adolescent rambling around the question. The simple ''we should get together some time, I'll message you' was completely out of reach of me in the moment I'd truly needed it. Now I'd gently spilled my guts either way, and they weren't going to go back in.

She smiled, and in doing so completely washed away my anxiety, she was so good at that.

"Please, stop talking" she said

She got up towards me.

"That's really sweet Mark"

Our lips met, silently, softly, for just a moment before they were separated and she looked into my eyes, foreheads touching, and smiled again.

III

It ended there. He took another look at the final, straggling, rum-soaked page and saw what looked like an attempt to continue that ended just shy of a full sentence. Last night Mark had clearly lost interest after the big kiss and had called that time to hit the hay. Maybe if he'd not insisted on pen-and-paper working for his fiction he could've kept going but thought that it would actually be disastrous had the same spillage occurred.

Mark looked at those last few words and the two-thirds of blank paper directly below them. As amusing as he'd found reading his somewhat creepy indulgence of his sadness he couldn't deny that he'd still felt that poignant void in his stomach whilst he read what might've been had he had his way. His lips touching Polly's, even in ink, was a tangible enough idea to make him contemplative of his own state. Another year of his own was nearly down the drain without having the guts to break past the electricity he'd felt around Polly.

Mark's phone buzzed and forcefully snapped him from the blank paper. A message from Jason, apparently it was another one, he'd been trying to get his attention at least half a dozen times since the early hours of the morning. Mostly the ramblings of the kind drunkard who becomes so innocently confused when intoxicated. The most recent was a coherent summation

[08:45] where'd you go last night Slimey?

Mark swallowed his angst and messaged back a stock response

Sorry dude, lot happening all at once nowadays [09:20]

He put his phone away and began his daily ritual of procrastinating the work he'd let pile up. The next hour was spent slowly shuffling between the bathroom and bedroom ending on letting the shower cleanse him of the odd feelings he'd spent the morning accruing. Then he left for work.

Mark had learned since he got his job to identify what kind of client he'd be working with before even meeting them. He'd read the job description from the office and based purely on the description he'd know.

First there were the boring people, the complete non-stating stories that managed to be too bland for the slowest of newsdays. These were the most common work, the easiest work, and by far the ones that lead to the longest work. Because like it or not there's a spot in that Local Oddities section that needs filling and if it's going to be filled with a few hundred words on a man who successfully ate a shoe then by gum that's what it's being filled with. Mark knew some people who thought that specific example should've fallen into a latter category but he's explained multiple times that beyond 'he ate a shoe for workplace bet' there's not a lot to say apart from rattling off more and more mundane details of the offender's life. There's no bottom to the mundanity of what can make it into that section, but the time he was told to write a story about an overly large truck that spent 40 minutes trying to negotiate a tight corner was probably close enough.

Then you get the crazies. When Mark would spend his days in disinterested journalism lectures he was never told that the job may well send you into the houses of people who let their 100 pet snakes run free with little regard for the safety of others. These were the worst not only because Mark was risking his life but more often than not the journalistic exploits would've been cut so short that the stories were unpublishable. He grew a habit of alerting his parents when he was being sent to somewhere like that in case he didn't return.

Then you get those stories that try to have some razzmatazz without the threat of death. Mark's favourite. These are the stories that one typically think of when they think of the mind-numbingly inane stories of local journalism, like interviewing a woman who was convinced her husband had transformed into a bottle of Nail Varnish Remover so was fighting for her right to marry it, or the man who did a poo so bad it broke the train toilet and caused mass delays, a lot of poo stories actually. There's a tinge of sadness to some of the stories but often times the person being interviewed are so confident and satisfied with their mundane achievement it's infectious. That, more than anything, was what Mark told people the best part of the job was. He was lying, it was how easy the work was, but friends don't generally appreciate you bragging that your job is too easy.

If you've ever looked at a newspaper and thought "what person thought this was news", there's a chance it was Mark. Or at least one of his superiors.

Today Mark was supposed to be interviewing a man who had tattooed himself into a Zebra.

Mark knocked on the front door of the Zebraman's house and turned to his assistant, a young Trainee called Hayley on her first outing, and explained the plan for the day.

He tried to sound professional "Okay kid, remember to treat every story like you're interviewing a man with 1 eye. Don't stare at the thing you're there to look at and let *them* establish how much we probe."

"What..?"

Mark sighed, "Just let them talk and look like you're writing things down. If we're quick we can leave before lunch"

"What kind of things do I write?"

Mark paused in the hopes the Zebraman would answer the door in time for him not to answer, the second it got too awkward a silence he admitted "...words".

The silence remained, Hayley went for a second attempt at the door but Mark looked at her disapprovingly. She knocked anyway, playfully sticking her tongue out at him in the process. It was far too early in the morning for him to be out of the house, only just past the 9 o'clock point, so all they had to do was wait long enough where they could rule out that Zebraman had just overslept.

"It's early days for you, you'll be jaded in due time" he cracked before pocketing his phone and eyeing his car. Another minute passed in awkward silence before Mark began to scribble something down and Hayley quizzically peered onto the notebook.

"What're you doing?"

"Leaving the Zebra we're hunting a note, a phone number and a passive-aggressive remark about not being in when he told us he'd be" He ripped off the page and stuffed it in the letterbox before turning on his heels and returning to the car.

"So all that was just pointless, getting all the way here? Really?"

"Unfortunately Hayley, not every thread gets tied up"

"That's not fair, was all this effort for nothing?"

"Yep" He left himself a quick note on his phone to return to the trail later and mentally signed out of work.

Mark offered Hayley a lift back to the headquarters, as he'd dubbed it, rather it was a tiny set of offices that were desperately trying to not go bankrupt before a majority of its workers could find backup jobs. But she turned him down instead taking advantage of the newly freed time to walk. He instead took it as time to go home, getting some rest before he needed to be back at work in the afternoon.

Mark was ultimately upset Hayley hadn't joined him because it would've given him an excuse not to think about last night. He sat in his own thoughts the whole ride, trying to parse the worst in him and the best in him, reaching for a compromise of both sides that would at least be enough to shut them up.

He'd spent a lot of his life trying desperately not to feel sorry for himself, he went through the standard suite of angsty phases growing up but always tried to resist the ever-tempting cycle of self-loathing. He was once told that life's short enough where any of your problems don't matter, at any moment some space phenomena that he didn't have the mind to understand could wipe him away like a whiteboard, then all that time worrying about job prospects or starting a family would've been a waste of breath.

Mark veered to the side, nearly siding into the car in the next lane before realising what he was doing and correcting himself sharply.

Every so often the little twitch in the back of his head, however, tells him he should care. The little twitch that always came back whenever he was around Polly. The kind of dull annoyance that was irregular enough to be of no concern in spite of feeling like it was. The whole drive home that twitch was there, biting away at the back of his mind letting him know that something wasn't quite right in the world. Maybe interacting with an actual human being had put into a bit of context, maybe his remark about loose threads had reminded him that he was actually capable of tying up that one, maybe it was something totally unrelated and he just so happened to be on the topic while it started. Either way, he figured he owed himself that finish it.

By the time he'd driven home it hadn't gone away, still there, being mildly annoying. He made his way inside and up to his desk The twitching subsided while he wrote.

"I really should be getting home"

"You should"

I gathered my few things together, I couldn't find the rum bottle anywhere but wasn't overtly bothered enough to spend more than a minute looking. The garden was what we'd've called a gentle mess when I was a child, can't take too long to clean up but that's a job for another time. If it comes up it'll come up naturally.

"Hey, Mark"

"Yeah?"

"Don't forget this, okay? It's good to finally have it out there"

"Don't worry, I won't, I'll get in touch soon to find a time we can get together, cool?"

We hugged one last time as before I left. In one night I felt like the world had left my shoulders. I'm not one to gamble, but I'd be willing to bet everything's going to be alright from here on out.

Mark punctuated the final line with a satisfying seal. It wasn't much, but a finished scene is a finished scene, regardless of circumstance, and that called for a proper ending.

Now it was in finished: it was cute, he thought, and only the slightest bit depressing upon further thought, the perfect thing to leave under a pile of other attempts at atmospheric writings to make the stack look bigger. It would probably need a name change if he ever wanted to tell anyone though, no one will ever look at it close enough to figure out the circumstances of its creation but if he left his own name in it it's not going to take a literary master to deduce it's maybe about himself. Regardless, it was done, Mark has satiated that itch of unease, and could now leave it.

He gathered up all the sheets, clipped them together, and placed them in his Graveyard drawer: the place where every one of his microstories sat when they were finished. He hadn't looked inside it in a long time now, every so often he'd debate looking through them for anything salvageable but the fact he knew he probably never would was why he knew it was just the right place for this one.

Mark closed the Graveyard drawer, mentally cleared himself of everything Paula, and moved on.

IV

It took a week to go past before Mark noticed the curiosity of the writing. The days had gone by interchangeably; essentially indistinguishable from any of his other days. Mark would spend his work time thinking about anything other than the task at hand and his free time endlessly running circles around the same few time killers that he'd always done. A lot of internet browsing, a lot of reading, mostly non-fiction this time of year since fiction is always best a treat for the summer. A bit of it was spent on research as well, acquiring general knowledge in case of future reports needing someone who's versed in local traditions or the workings of an outboard motor. At the very least, he thought, he'd eventually get a wide enough pool of knowledge to get on a game show.

Any other time was spent flirting with the idea of human interaction. Finding the time for people was easy since the indistinguishability of work and free time made procrastination easier to justify. The problem was always finding the people to fill the time. It always felt rude to pop up in someone's message window inquiring if they were busy or open to the idea of doing something. Not every time he'd fail to get past that rudeness, but enough times where he'd get actively annoyed at other people not being bored enough to be the ones to ask.

It was during one of these worry sessions of the rudeness of organising him and Jason's monthly mooch around the Red Arches Pub that Mark noticed it. A grim Saturday Morning where he was still required to work and had woken up in a fit of sneezing. In the week since the party his general lethargy had managed to spread to his immune system and it felt like his body just wasn't trying as hard to keep him in working order. He'd reached the point where he'd come to terms with the possibility that feeling like his head was stuffed with cotton balls was how the rest of his life was going to be.

As he reached down to the bottom drawer of his desk to find his laptop charger he noticed the drawer above it was wide open. The Graveyard's drawer was wide open. The Graveyard's draw was never left open out of a desire to keep its contents out of sight and out of mind. But this time it was leaning as far open as it could go and the contents were open to the world.

Most of the contents were gone as well. Mark pulled them out to confirm and only found a pair of paper-clipped bundles. Mark remembered there being around 7 or 8 exiled bundles in their last time he checked. But as he pulled out the drawer to look into the negative space for any loose sheets that had sprung out of their own accord it became abundantly clear that they most certainly won't there. The only thing to be found was the two that he'd taken out.

Mark skimmed through the first one, it was his own recount of the party again, cute, short, a few name changes away from being filler in a portfolio. Right down to the intentionally overdramatic final punctuation mark to seal it. Every page of it was there and accounted for.

The other bundle was odd. It was thin, only a handful of sheets deep. It was written in blue ink, an oddity considering Mark generally loathed writing in anything other than black. The handwriting was odd. He generally had good handwriting, at least people told him he had it, but the second bundle was writing in a much rougher style. It did somewhat resemble his own, but his own like he was in a rush or intentionally trying to make it look a little bit rough-around-the-edges. It also didn't turn page properly. Rather than a y-axis rotation between pages like a standard script, the back of each page was written upside down, making it difficult to decipher which part of it was actually the front page at a glance.

He only could conclude the writing was not his own, he read it anyway.

It's amazing, with how much I committed to memory of the moment I managed to jump the gorge between us, I'd let a lot of the time afterwards come together.

The first time we spoke after the party was the morning right after, I remember that clearly, I reread every message that morning a dozen times before I replied. In spite of the physical distance between the two of us being so much greater at that time, it was the moment that truly let it sink in to me that I'd managed to get even a step closer to her. I'd spent enough time in the past with the sense of loneliness that creeps in after the world conspires to remind one of it that I'd grown used to it, this was the first time I could remember where the sense came back. The fact it was so tangible, gone from a glow on the horizon to full-on sunrise that made the thought so powerful, even if it was just words on a screen.

I think I must've spent two hours in bed that morning and we only sent enough messages where it could've taken 20 minutes with a break for water. Worth every second though.

The first time we met in person after the event was actually by accident. Of all things, the discovery that I'd ran out of toilet roll took me on a trip out shopping, and since I was out I figured I'd take a trip to the nearby farmers' market to pass the time.

It was a standard affair, essentially a long row of pedlers and consumers walking and talking over a menagerie of Potatoes, Carrots, and other goods that were fine to show in their unglamorous, dirty glory. I'd always liked the idea of buying food from a place like this and I'd do it when I could, but it was never something that was on my mind when I ever needed them so I was mostly a stranger to the specific customs of the Market.

While I gormlessly looked at a pile of Sweet Potatoes debating if I remembered if they were actually growable in the UK I got a gentle tap on the shoulder. A tap on the wrong shoulder done intentionally badly enough where I knew to look the right way.

"Why hello there" she chirped. I turned around and immediately I lost interest in the sweet potatoes.

"Morning Paula, what brings you round this way"

"Me and Olivia were out to get lunch and figured we'd take a look at the local festivities" she gestured over her shoulder to a artsy looking girl in a beret trying not to give away how little she was interested in making my acquaintance.

"Hi, how you doing" I said, receiving only a nod of acknowledgement that was at least genuine enough to not come across rude, but enough for me to know that it was going to go no further.

"Are you here with anyone?"

"Nah, unfortunately not, I'm here on a bit of a tangent from some actual shopping I had to do and got caught up in the... charm? Let's go with Charm. It's just a pleasant place to be."

"I can certainly agree with that, it gives the place so much of an old-world vibe"

"Y'know farmers markets weren't started until '97, they're younger than us"

"Really?"

"Yep. Obviously farmers sold things since the middle ages, but an actual organized market like this? Only a few decades old."

"Wow, that's odd" Paula seemed genuinely interested but Olivia was beginning to impose herself to the side of us in the standard flank, favorite of the bored third-wheel trying to get the discussion to end. I noticed it, I doubt Paula did.

"I think your friend's bored"

"Yeah, we better be off, keep in touch though?"

"Certainly will!" I watched the two of them off, the long beige coat of Olivia being the final bit of them I saw before they became an indistinct part of the crowd.

Mark quickly searched for farmers markets. They were in fact established officially in 1997. In spite of it being the exact kind of useless trivia he'd remember for no reason other than to mock his ability to remember important things, he definitely didn't know that fact.

The next time we met was somewhere between accidental and properly planned. A few more days had gone by since the market encounter and it was late in the day when I got an stray message.

[18:49] Mark! I'm supposed to be getting a train to see my parents for the weekend but it's been cancelled and the next one isn't until eight. Going back home to kill time is unfeasible want to come down and kill time with me?

It seemed such a silly thing to request. After all, it was a friday night, and it was just late enough where going outside unplanned was off the table. But at its heart it was ultimately a call to not be left alone with oneself for too long and I sympathised.

Sure be like 10. [18:51]

I only lived a short drive from the train station so was able to be there quick enough to stay for an hour. I half suspect she didn't think I'd come judging by the element of surprise in her tired tone that evening. She'd chosen to sit on the platform bridge, letting the passing trains roll by underneath the two of us. When I arrived she seemed flustered, later telling me she originally thought she'd been late and the cancelled train was a wish gone wrong for the train to not leave at its proper time.

It was an quaint station, the station was oldschool, designed in the days of Steam for a schedule much lighter than the one it had to run to today. Because of that it was actually a relatively pleasant space, nice enough to where we could just burn the hour away peoplewatching with a couple of coffees.

She was the one who originally brought it up "You'll find that there's always just that little bit more going on that what you expect in places like this"

"What do you mean?"

"People like to forget a crowd is just a bunch of people, each one is there for a reason, there's no one there just because they really love being in a crowd"

"Never underestimate what people enjoy, Paula"

"Oh you know what I mean. Take a look at that guy" she pointed to a man standing on the platform below us. He was by himself on the platform. Not particularly doing anything, he'd spent the whole time they were there standing in place, occasionally shuffling around, with a bright purple suitcase and matching headphones around his neck. "Where d'you reckon he'd going"

Mark noticed the spelling error before he read the sentence.

I looked around to the boards "Look like station 2's going to Scarborough"

"You know what I mean, what's a guy like him going to a place like Scarborough with a bag like that for at this time"

"Probably going home"

"Who's he going home to?"

"Hmm?"

"He's clearly going there for a reason. Everyone here is going somewhere for a reason and it's not actually that hard to pick up why. You managed to figure out he's probably going home just by looking at him. People just don't want to, makes things too hard. It's easier to not think of other people like people"

I brushed it off as one of those things that sounded far more profound than it actually was but it was admittedly entertaining enough to pass the hour relatively quickly.

We made our way down to the platform, the platform opposite the purple man, as the continued person-watching dragged on to the point where her train actually pulled in.

"We still need to actually find a date idea" I hadn't even considered it a date, in spite of that being what it probably was, I couldn't say no to her confidence though

"I guess we do"

"Here's the deal, while I'm gone this weekend, find something for us to do. Make it snappy Marky".

So for the second time I found myself watching her seep into a crowd. I watched the train roll out as I zipped up my coat and prepared for the drive home, making extra note of the purple man on the way out, still standing there, waiting for his train home.

Mark didn't exactly know how to feel, lots of conflicting emotions ran around him as he read.

First, it was because he was sick, of course he was, he'd spent the past few days in a perpetual state of unwell. A state that wasn't ill enough to justify time away; he was mentally exhausted. But as he switched between the pages and traced over the words with his fingers he couldn't shake off the tangibility of what he was holding. He took another look in the drawer and confirmed that there was nothing there. If this was a hallucination it was a damn strong one. Strong enough to where he was willing to act under the assumption it wasn't.

Second, his reaction was to call the police. Someone had clearly come into his house while he was at some point in the night and... written? Not really written anything threatening or harsh or even directed at him. Just kind of written up some fiction and pocketed the rest for himself.

After a spotcheck of the rest of the house he came up with no better explanations. The rest of the bedroom was completely untouched none of the windows or doors had had their locks tampered with. There was no way someone would've been cocky enough to have slipped their way into the locks and have been courteous enough to re-lock them after they were done. The bathroom was untouched, the kitchen was exactly the same, nothing had been taken from any other cupcorards and nothing in the jumble of wires under the television were gone. His wallet, the big target of surprisingly mediocre value was still on the coffee table. Everything of any actual tangible value was completely untouched.

So the only thing that had actually been interacted with was the Graveyard drawer. It'd have to have been in the previous night, unless it was done earlier and the drawer just happened to have slid open during that night? Either way was unlikely but the first was incrementally less unlikely. Mark reread the original version, it was untouched, every word was the same it had been, at least as he remembered it. There was nothing new apart from the continuation.

The Third option option could be that it's a trick. Some form of next-level prank birthed from... someone. It would have had to have taken some insane skill and coordination to pull it off. But that seems equally unlikely still. Maybe for a TV show? Like he'd been signed up for some tricky new prank-show where they systematically mess with someone who they think is too sick and tired to notice. Apart from being a gross overstepping into his personal space it wasn't exactly the stupidest thing he'd ever heard a pranker-for-higher had done.

His phone buzzed to remind him he needed to get to work. All three possibilities were unlikely, and rather upsettingly, the least unlikely was the third. He kept an eye for any hidden cameras outside his front door peering into the house as he left.

V

Mark hated the thought of returning to his mundane work when on the cusp of a real mystery; the spark he had for work to begin with had been put out long ago after the umpteenth disappointment but since he knew there was a real mystery building up on his desk he struggled even more to care. So when he woke up that morning, fluey and cold, to remember he was being summoned to the local park to report on dog poo he could hardly describe himself as ecstatic to begin with. With what was happening though? He was positively resenting it

It was bitterly cold that morning. The sky was a sheet of unbroken cloud muting all the colours of the naturally vibrant atmosphere of a public park on a saturday lunchtime. Mark clasped his hands together and breathed into them trying to capture the warmth but couldn't shake the horrible cold.

"Y'know the reason it's so cold is because its so humid in Britain." Hayley interrupted, derailing his inner monolog "It makes it easier for the cold to get inside you".

Mark looked at her, somewhat disgusted by her continued zest and somewhat by his stomach rolling over itself.

"Good to know Hayley, that's really brightened up my day".

"Alright, no need to be snarky" she said, pulling her rucksack from the boot of her car, "What makes you…"

Mark sneezed.

"…fair enough. What's the mission briefing today?"

Mark wiped his nose then handed her a scrap of paper with the header 'IS THIS THE MOST LITTERED PARK IN ENGLAND?' which she blankly stared at.

"Really?"

"First journalistic principle, if you word a headline as a question, the answer is no. If it were true we'd say it were. Still we have to get pictures and find quote-unquote evidence"

Mark dropped his tissue on the floor after he'd finished clearing himself up and took out his camera. Lining up a shot of it against the tire of Hayley's car.

"Why'd you do that?"

Mark put on his faux-enthusiasm voice "Because we're here to make the news, not just report it", drawing up a smile that was equal parts earnest and disgust. The two began their circuit of the park after that.

"Why do you even do this job Mark?"

"Don't really know, Can't see myself doing anything else"

"You don't seem to enjoy it"

"Well thank you, Ms. Observant" He paused to carefully consider, concluding that an honest answer wouldn't do any harm. Plus it might end the train of thought faster than a lie "I mostly couldn't see myself doing a job that's samey. I liked the idea of the job as a kid, now I don't love it but it suits me"

"Oh... wasn't expecting such a serious answer"

"We'll take it for what it's worth then"

Lawborough Park was essentially one large circle around a lake with a few dozen yards of grass on each edge and a play area on one side. No one when designing the city actually wanted any greenery but a large body of water couldn't be casually relocated like the farmland that was probably nearby. While the headline was most likely untrue it was not a completely unfounded claim considering what they quickly found. While litter wasn't an abnormal problem on the paths. Essentially every bit of greenery without failure had multiple leavings from dogs in horrible piles scattered over them.

"It's so gross" Hayley commented

"Agreed, I don't get why people find it okay"

It was such a disgusting sight that it managed to circle back around to impressive. Eventually you'd think that it would get so dirty that dog walkers would go somewhere else but Lawborough generally lacked any other greenery so they must have to made do.

It's not to say the litter wasn't an issue. The paths were generally clear of generic rubbish because the wind was successfully blowing it into random corners and against trees, leaving decently big piles of rubbish in multiple clumps across the park. There was one especially large pile of plastic bags against the corner of a disused public toilets. All the bags were from the same supermarket.

"There must be dozens of them" Mark said, getting another photo of the mass of bags.

"I'd bet there's a reason for it. There's no way that many bags from the same place just happens out of the blue"

"Weirder things have happened. I guess I don't see why they'd dump bags like this willingly since they're not free anymore. I hope this is everything you dreamed of when studying Journalism"

"To be honest it isn't not what I expected. I was made well aware that not going into electronic journalism would lead to a lot of crap. I'm just surprised it was both literal and metaphorical"

"Litter and Zebraman aren't enough for you?"

"What happened with him, ever hear back?"

"No, and I'm determined to let that story die if he's not interested in it. Maybe he wound up regretting his decision or something but we've reached a point where it'd be rude for us to make the next move"

"What's this?" Hayley asked, having wandered off to the side during his tangent.

What she'd found was a disused statue buried between two hedges that had managed to grow after years of apathy from the groundskeepers. Hayley had to force branches out of the way to get a full view of it. Parts of it had either worn away or been stolen by vandals so the original shape was nearly unrecognisable.

"I remember these, the opening of these was one of my first reports in High School"

"What is it supposed to be"

"Some charity, can't remember what, set up 5 of these things at different points in the park. They're supposed to be Llamas. Each one was painted by a different local artist and you were supposed to try and find them all. It was a cute gimmick but, as you can see, they were kinda forgotten"

"Wow, what happened to the others"

"Oh lord, let me think..." it had been half a decade since he'd thought about them. It was odd that Hayley wasn't aware of them since there was only a few years between them. Perhaps he'd exaggerated the scale of their launch in his head "...this one's still here, another was moved into a museum in Doncaster of all places I'm pretty sure, I think the other three were taken by the original artists after the council announced they weren't going to be taking care of them any more. Did you really not know about these?"

"No, that's really neat. It would've been really cool to see this thing originally" The paint had mostly chipped away, exposing the rough material. But what little paint was left managed to remain incredibly vibrant, almost standoffishly bright compared to the muted pallet of the morning. Most of it was an incredible crimson, Mark could vaguely remember it having something to do with the suffragettes written on its sides. Now it was just a dilapidated Llama trying to fight off the elements.

"Yo Hayley, stay there"

Mark quickly darted around the corner back to the pile of plastic bags and took one back to the Llama. Carefully wrapping it over the statue's head he backed up as Hayley looked confused at him.

"We have our photo, now let's get going, there's a lot more park to tut at"

Hayley agreed and followed him. Hayley spent most of the time on her phone not conversing and certainly not taking in Mark's deep insights into the world of small-time journalism.

"Hey, there's actually a movement to refurbish and return those statues, that's so cool. That's a story we should be researching!"

"I can't argue with your enthusiasm Hayley, I'll give you that. you've got your foot in the door at the press, why not write it yourself?"

"That's not a bad idea Mark. They've got thing on Monday, I've not got anything tomorrow evening I might go"

"You mean Sunday right?"

"No, tomorrow, Monday"

Mark confusedly checked his phone, she was right. Today was Sunday. "I guess you're right. Shit I really wasted my free time"

"Sucks for you I guess"

As Hayley continued on her own train of thought, Mark had time to Dwell on her enthusiasm for the statues. He couldn't deny that it would be an interesting way to spend an afternoon trying to find the Llamas. He thought back to when they first launched. They were pretty impressive statues in spite of the glaring issue of why of all things they'd chosen Llamas.

That gave him an idea. He pulled out his phone and took a note.

I messaged Paula: 'Hey, they set up those Llama statues down in Lawborough Park we should go find them!'

He'll write it out neater, maybe flower it up so it seemed less rigid compared to the rest, atop a blank sheet of paper and leave it on his desk when he got home. Then wait.

VI

A few days later, he got his response.

[15:20] Awesome idea! I'd heard about that and was super interested in seeing them too! How about we do that like 11 day after tomorrow? We'll finish at 2ish, then I've got to sort out some stuff with my sister, then in the evening we dinner x

The weather was on the precipice of perfection. Every element of the scenery was on the cusp of being picturesque. There clouds were on the horizon in every direction but directly above me I could see into the endless blue. A single plane's contrail struck across the sky like a knife through butter and went nearly directly over the sun. Beautiful flowers bloomed along the sides of fences and the omnipresent bugs and bees that come with them were too busy doing their own thing to be a nuisance. I stepped out of my car into the light and was nearly blinded by the light, as glorious as it was at that moment I could tell it was raining the previous night as the concrete was bright enough to be dazzling.
I wasn't late, but by the time I'd gotten there Paula was already sitting on a bench in an elegant rose-patterned summer dress and a slick pair of sunglasses. She seemed so natural in that position I considered not even disturbing here, letting her become one with the gorgeous surroundings.

We found the first one immediately, hard not to notice something that was taking up a parking space. It was a brilliantly vivid Sky Blue, threatening to camouflage in the actual sky it was so well coloured. Along its underbelly and the side of its body was a delicately sketched alien cityscape, every building reached for the sky in corkscrews with a spiderweb of bridges and cables drawn between them in incredible detail. As up close as I could get without contact and still the details seemed to delve even deeper.

"It's supposed to represent something"

Paula laughed at my ignorance "Oh course it does, why wouldn't it?" she ran around the other side and peeked over the back of the Llama. "What do you think it means"

"Something about technology"

"No shit sherlock"

"Something to do with the future being bright. We like to think the future's going to go downhill but that's honestly never happened"

"I reckon it's the opposite, the bottom half is complicated and messy" I traced my finger along the skyline while she spoke "but the sky is clear, unmuddied"

"Interesting, doubt the bottom would be so detailed if that were the message thought"

"I guess we'll never know"

Paula leant in and gave the Llama a kiss on the cheek for a photo before excitedly stepping away to look for the next one.

The second was a lot harder to find, sunk off the path beneath a trio of horse chestnut trees. The Llama was painted a rough fuschia all over, with extra detail added to the face with thick black outlines resembling Makeup. Across the top of its head '1987' was written. All across the rest of the Llama were dozens of names written in a typewriter-eque font. Most of the names were written in uniform rows with the occasional name dashed in cursive written over the top. It gave the statue a very strange look from a distance, like it was covered in a thin haze.

"You recognize any of the names?" I asked, skimming over the list I recognized none myself.

Paula was around the other side and was looking equally bemused "No... Clare Short, James Wray, Eric Illsley, I got nothing it all seems like gibberish"

"Maybe if either of us were alive in '87 we'd recognize them"

"I don't know, it's a lot of names, there probably is a connection but it seems like way too many to be all one thing. Might be fun to look them up later"

I put on my best dramatic voice "If you remember nothing from this date then remember the name..." I pointed randomly onto the Llama's back "...Reverend Ian Paisley"

As I declared his name she began lining up for another photo of herself with the Llama, this time trying to look as cool as possible while posing with a fuschia painted Llama. As she did I quietly leant over and got the sliver of the side of my face in the top of the frame.

I found third one, it was disguised amongst the play area in the park. It was an insane fractal of rainbow henna. Absolutely dazzling to look at to a point where it became almost difficult to look at any one piece of it. Every time I tried to focus on a particular spiral or blossom of textures I'd get distracted by another branch of colour and lose track of where I was going.

"Woah..."

I patted the Llama on the head "I have no snide remarks about this one, it's just legitimately really damn cool"

This time she stood to the side of the Llama, trying to capture the whole insanity of the artwork in a single frame. She looked off into the distance, trying to seem dramatic and artsy, letting me again peek into the back of the frame as she took it. This time looking surprised at the visual cacophony of colour.

We nearly skipped over the fourth one it was so well hidden. It was carefully, neatly tucked just off the path between a pair of hedges. Poking its head just out it was easy to brush off as a part of the scenery. Just enough space had been cut out for a person to circle it. It was a beautifully rich Crimson all over. So forceful a colour the face of the Llama may as well have been smoothed over with a file. Along its sides were three elegantly painted ribbons. A purple on top, green on the bottom, white interwoven between the two. It was clear an incredible amount of care had gone into the ribbons and the Llama was used more as a canvas than an artistic medium

"What's this supposed to be?" I asked

"The three ribbons are from the suffragettes, this must be a tribute!"

"A tribute Llama?"

"Don't bite the hand that feeds you"

"I'm not sure that means what you think it means"

"Either way, it's neat. Is there any relevant local history to them that you know of?"

I bluntly shrugged, "Not my area"

This time she stood to the side, carefully getting the ribbons in the frame before posing. I felt it would be rude to crash that particular photograph.

Back at the parking area we realised we'd made a full circuit before finding the final one. I knew there were five to find but the four were evenly distributed so there was no obvious place for it to be. We peered over the still lake and confirmed that only three were visible

"There it is!" she exclaimed. I looked in the direction she pointed as far as I could go but found myself looking past the park and into the houses in the distance.

"Hand on, where we looking? In front of the houses?"

"No not there Mark, look!"

"How on earth could they have set that up?" I could just about see the 5th Llama, poking up from the Lake surface like a tiny whale I could just about make out the head of a Llama, it was Black, and was barely high enough to breath. All the four main Llamas were looking right at it and it was almost completely hidden.

"What a stupid idea, how are we supposed to see it?"

"Maybe we're not supposed to"

"Why make something to be seen then deliberately hide it?"

"Why make something to be seen?" she smirked, knowing I'd be absolutely incapable of firing back.

We walked up to the edge and stood with the toes of our shoes barely hovering above the water's edge. I started by trying to get a better view but ended up rather musing on the whole date. It can't've taken more than an hour and a half, maybe two, to find it all but it had felt like a proper fun little journey. It was cute, and had made the place that was ultimately just a random patch of empty space in the city that had lost its value into something worth visiting again.

"How do you plan on getting a photo of that one?" I asked.

She hummed gently like you could hear the disk spinning in her head before giving an overly dramatic snap. She ushered me closer as we both turned around and posed for the most humble of things, a Selfie. Taken from just the right angle that both of us got in with the tiniest speck in the background that was the Llama head.

With lightning speed she kissed my cheek when she took the photo. Just the right time to capture my expression of complete bewilderment on camera, forever immortalising the split second cocktail of emotions that comes from a surprise like that (or at least until the photo gets deleted).

"Part One of this date was a success I'd say" I declared to break myself from my own daze.

"Yep, I'll get the photos online tonight, they're all great"

"What you doing before we get dinner?"

"My sister needs help moving some stuff and she can't do it by herself"

"Why not, is she not as strong and capable as you?"

"No she's blind"

I paused, absolutely no clue how to either call her bluff or tastefully transition away from the joke. I ended up concluding the best course of action was to let out a noise somewhere between an 'oh' and a 'really'

"Yeah, so needs help moving things"

"I guess that's a valid thing to need help with then"

"It's whatever, you have to play with the cards you're dealt"

We managed to move past that dampener of the mood as we waved goodbye to the last Llama and returned home. I decided to be gentlemanly and walk her home, not just because my home was the same way. It was a beautiful enough day where *just walking next to her in a comfortable silence was more than enough. It was only a couple of minutes but I did really enjoy it. Something about the comfortable silence was alien to me, it's an underappreciated and rare occurrence that people often let slip by when talking about good experiences.*

We arrived at her house in no time and I said my goodbyes. After watching her return to her home I turned right around and headed straight back to the Park. Because I'd gotten so caught up on the wonderful walk to Paula's home that I'd forgotten I'd driven.

Mark finished reading. He'd asked for a response and had gotten it, yet the ecstatic joy he'd felt when he'd realised it had come for him while he was sleeping quickly turned uneasy when he realised he had no clue what to do with it. This time was the first time he'd taken a proper look at the Mark in the story. It seemed to resemble himself, or at least was some form of facsimile of himself, drenched in the flowers that always come with codifying the world in language. At multiple points when thinking about it he'd forgotten about Polly, it started as an indulgence of a wistful fantasy but it took no time become its own story entirely. Trying to think of it analytically was only putting unnecessary weight on his part in all of it.

After doing some research into the Llamas, finding pictures online of them from their glory days and beyond the one he remembered none of them matched the description he was delivered. In real life the Llamas were actually fairly banal, all the same brilliant red color with the symbols of different organisations that centred on some form of equality on the side. The only reason he'd forgotten them was how interchangeable they turned out to be. He remember each statue having a plaque that explained what they meant as well, it was in basically every photo, it seemed odd that they were left out.

He was still curious, but it had sank into an uneasy curiosity rather than his original whole-hearted embracing of the strange.

The initial buzz for the story had numbed fast, now he felt bizarrely guilty.

And he knew full well he had another date with Paula to sit through.

VII

While he waited anxiously for the next date to appear he set up his first real precaution against it. He placed a single small spy camera that he connected to his laptop pointing directly at the desk. It was relatively cheap and the stickyback didn't actually work so he had to place it on a shelf behind his desk, but regardless he could now reference whenever anything happened at the desk. After a few teething troubles he managed to get it all working properly. Then he waited. In the meantime he returned to his old vices.

One afternoon, while free of work, he decided to follow up on an old offer Jason made without even realising and called him in to the Red Arches pub.

The Red Arches was a strange place, the kind of pub that probably ran at an incredible profit through the combination of overpriced terrible drinks and being the only pub big enough where strangers won't recognise you if you go there regularly. A few years earlier he was told a story by a barmaid he was haplessly trying to flirt with that it was actually a massive money-laundering scheme for a couple of crooks based in Derby. Which, aside from the implication that Derby contains anything remotely worth being a criminal to attain, wouldn't surprise anyone.

Jason already had already ordered the first round by the time Mark arrived.

"I was wondering when you'd show up Mark" he said, getting up from his seat to move his jacked off the only other chair

"We've been over this Jason, you don't have the right to act like I'm late when you arrive early. I can't help that you're such an alcy that you can't wait to order"

"Whatever, I'm surprised, why the sudden call for pub?"

"Ever feel like you're living through the world's least-impressive trainwreck?"

"You're not at work now Mark, you can stop dressing everything up like it's important. Now, in english?"

"Life's weirding me out right now, and I'm actively trying to not dig the hole any deeper"

"That still doesn't sound english"

"I kinda need to be out of the house for a while and knew you're always free because you never seem to work"

"Hey man, electricity is a risky business. Sometimes it takes me like a week to find out what the right equipment for rewiring a vintage light bulb is. I can't help that fact"

"Oh god, tell me you're not that kind of Sparky"

Jason laughed a surprisingly nonreassuring laugh "Like you're a saint"

"Yeah, but what I do might not burn my house down"

"If you think about it: what I do might not burn *my* house down. Unless a particularly arson-ey person decides they don't like the fact that I can't magically install a million plug sockets in one room"

"Do people really ask for stuff like that?"

"You'd be surprised Mark, I told you about the idiot I dealt with last week"

"You mentioned him, you mean the guy who broke the plug so just jammed the wire into the socket?"

"Yeah, that moron, he called me in because he was surprised his fridge wasn't working after plugging a bare wire right into the ground hole. He's lucky he went there because knowing his train of thought he probably would've tried licking it"

"I remember being taught plug wiring at school, they must still do that, plus we have the internet anyway, what kind of person doesn't think to try that in 2018"

"It's mental. The world is full of stupid people trying to find the stupidest way to kill themselves"

Mark could certainly attest to that, he thought, while excusing himself to buy the second round of drinks. When he first got his job at the Press he briefly went through a period of actually reading the paper until transitioning into buying them for archiving his own articles. For that brief time he kept notes of his favorite absurd stories that stuck out to him as particularly eyeopening. This stories varied from legitimate controversies that were worth far more space than a middlingly-successful local paper could give to the extreme achievements in mundanity that soon became his forte to stories that were pulled straight out of a stand-up-routine.

Mark flagged down the barman and ordered two pints. One story that stood out in his memory was the story of a pair of golf enthusiasts. After driving a ball straight off the course one of the two went out to find it, after failing he yelled to his his friend to drive a similar one so he could watch the trajectory.

Surprisingly enough, the ball managed to strike him right in the face, knocking him out. He turned out okay in the end which was enough justification for Mark to find it funny. But he knew stories like that were absolutely everywhere.

He payed for the drinks and returned to Jason, intending to tell the story of the golfing buddies

"While you was up there I remembered. This Saturday the missus is hosting one of those dinner parties where she gets her single friends together and tries to mingle them. She's letting me bring a plus one. Can I put you down?"

"Ehh... I'm not sure. You know I can't stand her friends either I'm not sure what I'd add"

"But I don't want to be stuck with them by myself"

"I get what you're saying but..." he needed a lie quickly, Mark found his mouth a second ahead of his head "..I think I have a date that night" of all the things he could've said in an attempt not to lose conversational momentum he came up with that one.

"Oh really, so you've found a bird and now you're abandoning your friend. Typical Slimey"

He could tell it was teasing, he'd never seen Jason actually offended before and he knew this wasn't it. Mark knew Jason was as bad at picking up on lies as he was at lying so he felt comfortable gently twisting the truth to stop himself having to explain his current situation.

"Yeah, kinda, it's complicated"

"That doesn't sound like something that can be complicated"

"You'd be surprised" I fake-laughed and took another drink. Hoping it was enough for him to stop probing.

"Anyone I'd know?"

"Umm... no. She works at the Press.

"Blegh, another wordy type.

"Yeah she's been fucking me around a lot. Hoping to try and wrangle it into something coherent sooner rather than later" he considered that less than a lie.

"Well don't let her. No healthy relationship involves fuckery in anywhere other than the bedroom and occasionally the kitchen"

"Jesus Jason, when did you ever come out with such half-competent advice?"

"TV mostly" In a second they were both jostled from their seats. A single wave birthed from a dozen sources triggered in instinctive reaction in them both to flee as they leapt from their table and made it what felt like half way across the room in an instant. Jason was slower to the mark, having more to move and more alcohol dulling his senses he managed to get out of the area slow enough to not be completely safe. Before either had properly registered what had happened Jason was compressing the back of his hand to stop the bleeding.

Still on instinct, Mark took his phone from the tabletop and checked it, it had recieved near direct impact but managed to remain unscaithed through some minor miracle.

By the time he'd rebooted and the higher parts of his brain whirred back into motion most of the pub had also heard what happened and were watching, either quizzativly or worridly.

A man, a woman, and a third person neither of them got a good look at had been at the Red Arches the same time as Mark and Jason. They'd been there significantly longer Mark would later discover, Jason said he'd noticed them being rowdy when he first arrived. They seemed to span the age range between them, in most contexts he'd've assume they were from three different generations, but for some reason they were all drinking heavily together. Mark thought back to what Paula had told him, they almost certainly had an absolutely fascinating story why they were there, a story Mark will never even get a chance know.

In their rowdiness one of them, the ambiguous one, threw a punch at the man. The man threw a punch back. The woman tried to break them up, still holding her glass. That act of heroism earned her a punch in the face: throwing her back and causing her to release her glass into the air. Which made an impressively direct path onto Mark and Jason's table and shattering between them on impact.

Apart from a shard flinging past and cutting the back of Jason's hand they'd both managed to jump free in time. The bleeding wasn't too bad, but it was enough to where at least three random other patrons had offered tissues for wiping it.

Most of the attention was still on the trio, who had been forcefully

Mark and Jason left too at that point, not out the same door as the fighters, and took a breath. They'd been offered apologies from the bar staff which Mark found strangely meaningless and decided that they could have bartered for free drinks to replace what was spilled in the scramble but had remained courteous enough let it slide.

"Jesus Christ it's dark, what time is it?"

Jason checked his watch "Like 7:30"

"Crap, I could've sworn it was way easier, how long were we in there?"

He shrugged, then cheekily grabbed my shoulders "Let's head over to Wagon & Barrell. They have a pool table and hopefully less nutcases"

"Don't you want to get something for your hand? It doesn't look bad but it doesn't look ignorable"

"I'll get some loo roll when we're there. So the less you stall the more time I'll be bandaged up"

"Can't argue with that"

VIII

I know I should've expected something of this calibre when we decided to go for an evening dinner but I'd never expected somewhere so french. The whole restaurant was draped in an exquisite atmosphere that felt almost oppressively refined. The gentle hum of conversations scattered in the sea of tables were doing a lot of work in making me feel like I wasn't completely out of my water. Everyone was dressed in the finest they could, a majority of the men were in full-blown suit-and-tie which made my own attempt of a dress shirt and smart trousers feel inferior. Paula perfectly judged the tone, a beautiful green dress that looked fresh off the latest supermodel.

"I won't lie, this is totally a new experience for me"

"To be honest I've never actually been either, I got the recommendation from my sister, she's taken quite a few of her dates here before"

"Can't argue with that, it certainly looks like she's got taste" I winced at how accidentally rude that remark might've been but Paula seemed to not notice.

We were taken to our seat by the waiter and left to our own devices. We were essentially against a wall so much of the noise was projected away from us so we could both get lost in our own world. We both took to our menus.

"Do you speak any French?" Paula asked, looking completely bemused by half of the options. I, rather, got completely lost in the prices. I was lucky to where I had a little spare cash at most times but I'd never had a chance to spend so much on something that, by design, wouldn't last more than a few hours.

"I'll take that as a no" she laughed, putting the menu back down with a force enough to put me on edge. "Good luck"

Every item was a combination of syllables I had no clue how to approach. Various bits of structure remained from lessons over half a decade in the past but I still had no clue what that c with a line under it means, nor how to pronounce a word with a 'dc' in it, I swear half of it was made up to confuse people like me.

The waiter arrived back in what felt like no time as I was still deliberating. I panicked and in the least clumsy french I could muster I ordered the first thing I could that looked like a main course "Broiled Espadon À La Niçoise please? And a bottle of house red"

Paula ordered as well in a far more convincing accent and the waiter took our menus.

She leant over slightly and mouthed to me

'any idea what you just ordered?'

I leant over back

'honestly no'

'that sucks, i just copied you'

I was absolutely gobsmacked by her trust in me since I'd now doomed us both to ordering something worth quite a lot of money essentially on a dice roll. She found it no bounds of hilarious, evidently not carrying the same worries as I was and was still smirking about it when he waiter returned with our drink.

"I never had you down a wine man, Mark"

"Honestly not" I said, pouring us each a glass "I don't hate it but wouldn't choose it unless the situation called for it" I held up my glass as if demonstrating my domain and she nodded, satisfied with my answer. I'd loosened up considerably now the we'd ordered, now the anxiety of impressing with my culture was gone I could enjoy the ambiance more.

"You even been to a place like this before? You said you'd never been here but anywhere similar?"

"For mine and my sister's 18th birthdays we went to Edinburgh and London respectively and both weekends involved eating at a place like this. Beyond that I'd never felt like I'd come across the right situation to justify the occasion"

"Why'd you pick it for me then?"

"Your idea with the Llamas was so amazing that I felt like I needed to top it" the sarcasm was obvious, yet still playful.

Resulting in what felt only like an answer that dodged the question.

"What about you?"

"Nah, like you I never found the right occasion, and my mum doesn't really enjoy environments like this so no one ever saw fit to take me. It's hard to justify a place like this on the wage I'm on"

"It's a bit ritzier than I expected from her descriptions I'll tell you that much" she saw fit to quickly change the subject away from the restaurant "What's working for the papers properly like? See yourself moving on from it or are you in the for long haul?"

"I don't see myself going anywhere soon. The medium's not as close to the grave as people think it is, I think at least. The news is just entertainment at the end of the day and there will never be a world where people want less entertainment. I'd like to move on to more important stories and maybe gain some of that 'proper' credibility but there's plenty of time for that"

"No big dream job?" She asked, seemingly genuinely inquisitive to an unusual degree for a question that seemed mundane to me.

"Being content with where you are is a greatly underrated feeling I say. Sure I'd love to achieve the kind of greatness that earns your name in the history books but that's so incomprehensible a goal that I just don't care. If everyone left a mark we'd be dealing with an incredibly dirty history"

Paula seemed genuinely unsure of how to respond. Threatening to get lost in the middle-distance contemplating what I'd said before I roped her back. Since she was so curious about my own I figured it was fair for her provide her half of the story.

"Why do you teach? That seems like the kind of job you have to be in it for the long haul"

"I like the idea of having a job where it's immediately obvious who you're helping, if that makes sense, and unlike

nursing or policing, teaching was the only one I was actually qualified to do."

"What're the children like?"

"Kids are kids, what can I say really. They manage to be heartwarmingly earnest or arseholes. And when they're arseholes it's hard to tell if it's because they're genuine or just haven't got a full grasp of things yet. That's why I could never do secondary school, by that point being an arsehole is in their character"

We both take the natural pause as a chance to sit back and appreciate how relaxed we'd become. I couldn't speak for her but I'd unwound considerably already. In spite of the dozens of patrons whose various voices were floating in the air no one in the room was actually paying attention to me apart from Paula. And the waiters I suppose, but they were processing people by the hundred daily and even the largest brain couldn't remember all of those details.

Our meals arrived shortly after. I had no idea what it was, some fish-based thing. I was never any good at identifying fish when they were alive but cooked and served in a menagerie of garnish it seemed even more homogeneous. It was beautifully constructed, and I felt like anything less than a delicate dissection to see the contents would be rude to the dead fish. My hand movements were more akin to a renaissance painter than a modern day hungry man.

Paula took to the meal immediately, skipping the investigatory phase and going straight for the assault. Not even stopping to size up where one should approach from "Any clue what it is?" I asked.

"Nope. Tastes very south-of-france. More mediterranean than the channel"

"I adore your confidence. If this were just me I'd spend half an hour dissecting it before I had the guts to go for it"

"Fuck it, go for it, and I don't even need to pardon my french in here"

I skewered together as much as I could without making it too much to handle and went for it. It was surprisingly sweet. Definitely a fish of some kind, maybe Monkfish of all things? I don't really know the difference between white and red meats in land animals and couldn't remember if the same was true of fish. I swallowed and mulled over what I'd just eaten.

"Ever realise too late you know absolutely nothing about food?"

Paula elected to cover her mouth when she spoke rather than to finish what she was chewing "The trick is to not look like you know nothing. That way no one will question it unless you draw attention to it"

"You mean exactly like I just did?"

"Yeah, don't do that"

Paula finished in no time and I took considerably longer, mostly because every bite I got caught up on trying to pin what exactly it was. It was a very odd experience eating something with no concept of what it was and I found it hard to push pass the guessing game. By the time I'd finished Paula was refilling her wine.

"What do you think?"

"I liked it, just not sure I could parse much of it. I guess I like my food a bit simpler. I'd say I probably wouldn't order it again but I still don't have much of a clue what it actually was"

"I'm not much into fish, so not for me either. You should've picked a better meal Mark"

"Hey, I'm not the one who mindlessly copied someone else's order!"

She shot me a playful glare and laughed.

"What about you Ms. Cultured, like it?"

"I really enjoyed it! My Dad's a bit of an artist when it comes to cooking so I've got quite a wide pallet"

"Must've been fun having that kind of creativity coming from a parent"

She paused "Did you not have anything like that?"

"No, my parents worked a lot. I'm a bit of a stereotypical neglected only child except not as harsh as that trope implies. They cared, it's just their idea of caring was working super hard to give me a good life, so I spent a lot of time by myself. 'Cause of that all the creativity in my house came from me, and kids like me didn't put that creativity into food"

"What kind of things did you put it into?"

"Y'know, stuff. Stuff kids do, I drew, I destroyed things, I wrote things, I made things. All that jazz"

"Interesting you'd go somewhere so, academic? Is that the right word? Kids like that usually end up the creative artsy types. Musicians, Poets, Film makers, unless I'm vastly misinterpreting it journalism wouldn't fall under that"

I laughed at the thought, some of the things I'd encountered on the job were infinitely stranger than anything some artist would conjure "Like I mentioned earlier, things like that are a nice dream but there's no substance to a dream. Achieving something like that is almost predestined in a way. Don't think I've ever felt like I was interesting enough to write anything destiny would call for"

"What do you mean?"

"I guess I'm more concerned for myself than what I do. I try to enjoy life, when that becomes so easy it happens by itself I'll focus on something bigger, but while it's still tough I'll focus on that"

"You're a little rough around the edges Mark, but I don't think that's a bad thing. Since I've known you you've never struck me as someone anyone would want to do worse, why not put yourself out a bit more?"

"I just hate getting in the way I guess, I enjoy being around people and putting myself out there but I'm a bit too easily convinced I'm not needed"

"Not needed?"

"Like, take a time back when I first got my first job. Everyone already had friends so I just didn't bother trying to make any. Eventually I made friends but I was fine just turning up and doing whatever"

"Life is about more than surviving sometimes Mark"

"I know that more now, just hard to change my instincts"

Paula catches the attention of a waiter hovering in the area and motions for the bill. We both made a concerted motion to finish our drinks and the rush of alcohol caught of off guard.

The waiter returned, a different waiter than the one who'd taken her request for the bill, and motioned it to us. Without hesitation Paula placed a card on the dish and it was taken away.

"Woah..."

"Don't pretend you didn't skip a beat when you saw the prices. I'm not letting you off, you'll owe me next time, but I'll take the immediate hit"

I didn't feel particularly like arguing in spite of how I disagreed "At least did you not at least think to check if that was the right bill"

She shrugged as the waiter came back, a third waiter, the original one who brought us to our seat at the start of the night, returned with her card.

"Well then, Shall we be gone, M'lady?"

"Only if you promise me you'll never say that again"

IX

Mark couldn't remember returning home that evening, Jason's uncanny ability to pass on his heavyweight alcohol consumption to his peers was enough to black him out. The night fades out somewhere in the Red Arches and doesn't return into view until he's back home. He remembered something about locking the door, fumbling with the key through his beer goggles. He remembered trying to make his way to the toilet and getting lost in his own home on the way. But above all he remembered the instantaneously sobering realisation that while he was gone his desk had reshuffled itself another time. Since then he'd read it at least daily since it appeared. Whatever was doing it was being tricky enough to never be around the same time as himself. Even more so tricky enough to do it while he was blacked out, so all his memories could only be partitioned into before and after it showed up.

The next few days passed Mark by uneventfully. Any other times than when he'd find something new on his desk seemed to fade away with time. Putting himself in a stasis for days where all he would do is eat, sleep and sit around waiting to catch the words appearing on the paper.

The Mark on the paper felt more of an uncanny recreation of himself than a reflection. He knew enough french to know what he'd ordered was a fish-based salad before it arrived, he knew who Ian Paisley was. That was whatever. Even the accuracies weren't too concerning. The only child stuff and his opinions on Wine were mundane enough details where they were within a decent guess's range after a little exposure to him.

What worried him was the undefinables. The things that sat around him that didn't seem true but couldn't be easily logiced away.

He'd skimmed over the footage of the camera from around the dinner date and had come up empty. Only endless footage of a desk with a mysterious wreath of papers sitting silently in the drawer and occasionally the back of his own head sitting down to check his laptop or comb through the details of the earlier parts of the half written of the story. Trying to find a hidden code or small detail that would give him a clue as to the author but was never able to come to a conclusion.

Mark often wondered in that time how people would react if he told them what he was doing. Vanishing for days on end to observe a slowly growing semi-competent manuscript. Whether he'd end up concluding Ghosts or Magic or a corruption of the laws of nature he knew he'd end up sounding like a madman, the kind of person lumped in with the doomsday preppers and the touched-by-an-angel crowd: desperately trying to let others in on the magical breakthrough they've made in discovering the fundamentals of reality.

A few times he tried researching his situation, trying to find a long-forgotten forum post or an obscure video buried in time where someone was raving about a similar issue. But under the thousands of alien abductions and ghost sightings he couldn't find a story like his own that matched well enough. Even posting a few more times himself and never getting anything more than a few token acknowledgements of the strangeness of it from the implicitly disinterested.

The time eventually tricked away enough for someone to take notice. Mark found himself sitting on his bed, looking up the street, entranced by the passing of the cars when he noticed someone walking down the road he recognized. He couldn't remember when in the day it was or what else he had done beyond staring at the cars because this was the first thing of note. He watched the person make their way past the other walkers and cross the road to his side. He watched the long purple coated figure walk right up to the outside of his house and a beat after being too close to see he heard his doorbell ring.

He found himself running to the door, he wasn't sure why.

He was met by Hayley, somewhat startled by how forcefully he opened the door and unsure of what exactly to say to him.

"Oh, Good morning Hayley. You okay?"

I picked up my jacket from the Coat Check and tentatively turned to Paula. "Tonight's been a lot of fun"

"It has been" she smiled as she gently swayed on the spot, "Sorry, I always forget how much Red goes to my head", attempting to suppress a giggle at her own accidental rhyme.

"Yeah, yeah, I'm doing alright. Are you yourself okay?"

"I'm fine, why wouldn't I be fine? Just needed a few days off to sort some stuff".

"It's okay, you sure you're fine to drive?"

"Ha, no. I got the bus. I half expected this to happen"

"Umm... what am I expected to take from the admission you expected this?"

Hayley looked at me, compared to her, pristine and proper in a carefully chosen outfit; Mark was a mess, unsure of what shirt he was wearing or when his trousers were last washed.

"Okay, I look pretty bad, but it's only because you got me up so early, haven't had the time to get ready yet".

She pouted at me playfully, twirling her hair and trying to come up with an optimal answer.

Bemusedly, she checked her watch and Mark felt sheepish without even knowing.

"Have you just gotten up"

I saved her from having to think "Sure you're in the best state for a bus then? I can give you a lift if you'd like"

"That's super sweet, but you don't have to go out of the way." she pondered to herself for a moment, letting her eyes wander into the ether "let's compromise, I'm like a 10 minute walk from your house, how about a lift there?"

I threw my keys a few inches in the air and caught them, "sounds like a plan".

"Err... kind of. Just not eaten yet"

Mark had tried to make that as casual a remark as he could but Hayley look shocked. "Bloody Hell. 1:30! Get your coat dude, I'm buying you breakfast".

The ride was a quiet one but a comfortable one. The radio hummed a quiet medley of the 80s and we admired the view of the nicer side of Lawborough at twilight. It was that perfect time, late in the evening where the day was over and the night had yet to begin. Aside from the stray late-shift workers and a few cars, everyone else was either at the point of happily finishing their days or preparing themselves for their night. At one point Paula pointed out the student bar was empty, joking about how we're in the magical time between the philosophy students and the sports teams.

I considered intentionally taking a longer route to prolong the comfortable chitchat but by the time I could've put it into action we were close enough to where she'd notice. I ended up parking in the middle of a tangent about the corner shop her friend's dad owned.

As we got out of the car I looked at my awkward terrace house and considered his next actions carefully

"Mind if I come in for a quick drink?" Paula said, completely railroading my train of thought.

"Uh sure"

Inviting herself in she picked up one of Mark's coats and threw it on him. Reluctantly he listened to his empty stomach and accepted her offer.

I didn't even think if that was what I wanted but after being caught of guard I twitched out that answer. She might've read it on his face but she didn't care. She lightly jogged around the car to my side and gestured to lead the way. Before I knew it I was unlocking the door and showing her into the living room where she'd plucked a glass of water seemingly out of thin air.

Hayley took him to a nearby pastry shop, a local shop that could never have been running at a profit but never actually shut down.

"So how've things been at work."

Electing to sit on the floor with her back on the sofa I joined her across the room with a bottle of beer out of the fridge. We sat in a similar comfortable silence as she began flicking through her phone, tying up the final bits of the day she'd be putting off. I tried to be polite but I couldn't stop myself from looking at her as she did. I thought to compare her to an acquired taste but it's too easy to get tired of a flavor. I'd not become sick of her, the elegant grace she had started the night on was gone: now as she sat cross-legged squinting ever-so-slightly at her screen she had a more cozy demeanor that was equally intoxicating.

"Things seem okay. Rose came back from leave right as you left so things are a lot less chaotic now."

"That's nice."

Eventually she did turn off her phone and turn to meet my gaze, she gave me a sideways smile and laughed to herself.

We stood around awkwardly as I looked for what I wanted to eat, it all looked so good, I'd forgotten what proper made food tasted like and my stomach was threatening to jump out.

"What's your deal Mark?"

"Have you done anything about this"

"What?"

"Hmm..?"

"What makes you Mark? What's your deal?"

"Something's clearly wrong with you"

"I'm working on it, it's no one thing so I've got to see where it goes until I do anything else"

"I thought I told you a lot at dinner today"

"That's the public-Mark, all the nice things you put in the shop window to bring in customers, what's going on behind the counter?"

"Still not sure I follow to be honest"

"Okay, I'll lead" She pushed herself forward into the centre of the floor and patted in front of her for me to move forward. We ended up sitting close enough where we were nearly touching. "When I was 16 I got kicked out of school for cutting another girl's hair in class"

"That's... why?"

"Because she insulted my own hair so I wanted her to know what bad hair truly was"

"That makes sense I suppose. Flu can get to you like that I guess"

"Tell me about it. Tried quarantining myself as you can tell"

"I guess"

She blushed, running her fingers through her bangs. I reached out to touch her cheek but hesitated too long before she looked back up "So, what's your deal Mark?"

I laughed. "My school days were kinda boring, my dad was super pushy about me studying science though", I pondered on that, "I guess he kinda regretted not ever doing much with his own life".

"What do you mean?"

Hayley walked to the counter.

"What do you want?"

"When I was super young, 6 or 7, he was diagnosed with something, I honestly don't know with what though. So I guess he was trying to live vicariously. Either way he died when I was 11"

"I'll pay, don't fret"

"That's so sad."

"It is but don't get caught up on it. Regardless of how much I hated the stuff it was good to get so much time with him before he died"

She leaned in and placed her hand on my cheek "Maybe he just wanted to be extra sure you'd turn out smart even without him"

"Okay then..." she turned to place her order as Mark looked around. There was a small screen in the corner, a CRT that probably hadn't been moved in over a decade on some nature documentary.

"Ever follow up on our Zebraman?

I looked down and chuckled to myself, I'd never thought of it like that before and it did strike a chord in me.

The game continued *"I don't think I ever got over my first boyfriend, it's ruined a lot of my other relationships".*

Hayley visibly tensed up before answering.

I nodded, beckoning her to continue but she didn't.

"Presume that was a long time ago now"

She sniffled "Maybe 8 years now. Every boyfriend I've had since I've been comparing to him."

"He must have been quite a special person then".

"He died"

"I'm sorry, what?"

"Yeah, he died"

"You'd think so, that's why I'm not sure if I'm over him, I'd compare boyfriends to him and they'd often come up better. But I never stopped the comparisons. Every time something great would happen or a new feeling came up I was still comparing how much better it was than him"

"That's Okay. I'm not sure I'd ever say I had a proper girlfriend. I think I was always too comfortable with being friends that I never got around to trying. Comfortable or afraid."

"Or both?"

Mark paid the woman behind the counter who looked at him with a curious look. The same way he imagined he looked when pretending he wasn't listening in to an argument.

"Like, after we were meant to be there?"

"Hey, this is supposed to me by moment!". She found that funny. Trying not to show how pleased she was by how she'd thrown me.

"Even so. Maybe both. There were girls I knew who we technically were a couple, I think, but I've never made a conscious effort to reach that stage".

"Why not?"

"Comfort, or fear."

Hayley grimaced "It's a bit bleak, he slipped in the shower the night before. No one discovered it until I tried getting ahold of his family to ask where he was."

"...shit."

"That's Okay." She paused to think of another.

"I always resented my sister being blind. I don't know why, well I do, but you know what it's like when you're a kid, feeling like attention is your birthright"

"Oh yeah, I am well aware of that fun time in one's life"

"I was bad about it. Real bad, I let her know all the time how bad I feel about it and she's never once held anything against me. Now I only get mad at her because she doesn't get mad at me"

"Yeah, we could've been the first people to find him"

"To be fair, that's not really true, we were never realistically going to get in there. Plus the postman probably had come by as well and he had the same chance we did"

"I know, it's just sad."

He took his change and the two of them walked outside.

"Keep in mind he was like 65 though. He was certainly old. It sucks but it's not the worst thing in the world" Mark didn't expect that to come out as abruptly as it did, he could tell Hayley was processing how to take it "Maybe, I'm a bit too drained to correctly emote about that so give me a break"

"At least you had a sister. Being an only child sucks".

We let the silence linger on that remark, gently reverberating out the door and into the rest of the house. I hadn't realised how close we'd gotten. One or both of us had been drawing in closer to where we were sat between each others legs. Any closer and our bodies would have to be touching. I could feel her breath, I could see the twitching in her eyes as the looked at me looking at her. I was unable to move out of worry I'd shatter the moment like porcelain. Knotted together, talking about our problems.

The walk back to Mark's house was mostly silent. The two not really sure where else to take the conversation and too busy with their meals to care.

"What are you going to do now?"

"Not sure."

"That's Okay".

Mark unlocked his door, deliberately stepping in a way to give Hayley the smallest window inside as possible.

"Thanks, it's done a legitimate bit of good seeing you today"

"It's fine, lots of people were concerned for you but no one was actually checking and I figured someone needed too"

"Like I said, not really in a good place for expressing emotion, but it really has been good. I'll owe you a favor if you're sick"

"Let's go with that" she smiled. "That or promise me you'll shower and get dressed before you continue your quarantine, you called it?"

We continued to stare into each other. I know where this is supposed to be going, I know that soon one of us will have to do something to take us from our painting-like trance back into the real world. I ask myself what I should do next, do I move closer?, do I end the night on this dizzying high?, do I simply wait and see if she has a better idea? I was watching her glide her eyes over me. She, just like me, was impatient for one of us to do something. I took a deep breath and leant a fraction of an inch closer, just enough for her attention to be captured by it.

Mark looked down. He was in his pajamas, he'd spent the whole time without even noticing. The image of the two of them; her wrapped smartly up for the surprisingly bitter cold, and him in a pair of long-forgotten PJs that were half-too-big-half-too-small was enough to put away any good feelings he'd pulled out.

Instead of speaking I overexaggerated a look at the wall clock and watched her follow. It was late. Too late for her to walk home. Too late for either of us to back down now.

"Oh god, I'm so sorry. No wonder the cashier looked funny at me. I look like I've just gotten out of a home"

Her eyes told me she'd stay. We stood up together, fumbling slightly due to how close we were sitting, I threatened to fall at one point but she managed to grab me fast. I wish I were smooth enough to have intentionally do that because it resulted in her arm being around me, than her other found its way around me as well. It felt like the most natural place in the universe to be, of course it was, some things are just designed that way.

Hayley looked innocently condescendingly at him "Take care of yourself Mark". She waved goodbye and he waved back, watching her down the street and into a nearby ginnel.

Everything I've ever done was in aid of getting myself here.

The next thing I knew we were in my bedroom getting undressed, I bit my lip when I saw her, I like to think she did the same. She was human, I'd never truly thought of it, she was a woman, she was beautiful, I was embarrassed by myself but she caught me before I could be too timid and kissed me softly on the cheek.

Feeling the ever-so-slightest bit reinvigorated he hatched his self-improvement plan. He went upstairs to check the desk, nothing had changed, even after double checking the draws and notes nothing new had appeared.

Mark got changed and bagged up his pajamas, they needed shifting anyway and he figured this brief window of cheeriness was the best time to get it done. Putting in his headphones for the first time in weeks he turned on to whatever was last on and picked up a few other things in need of the landfill.

When Mark opened the bin to drop the bag he caught a glimpse of what was inside, nothing, mostly. The bin had been taken a few days ago and he hadn't put anything in it since so the mostly dead space was understandable but neatly placed inside was a small pocketbook.

Only a few dozen pages thick, it looked like other pages had intentionally been torn out.

Mark dropped his bag and in doing so accidentally tugged out his headphones.

Reaching into the bin, trying to ignore the residual smell of rubbish, he opened the pad.

We didn't end up sleeping together, not the colloquial meaning of the phrase anyway. I wasn't particularly interested. I was too happy to be there with her, in my bed, holding her in my arms, sharing our body warmth, letting the voices in my head sing a choir, sending me to sleep, feeling the softness of her skin, the crease left by her bra, the thousand subtleties that are lost at a distance, Paula. Two hearts in one bed.

He read up to the last word in the first sentence then ripped out the last page, then the page before that, he kept going until the book was no more than a scattered collection of loose sheets. He watched them drift away, getting tangled in the trees or escaping beyond the horizon, any emotions he threatened to feel where suppressed by an oppressive sheet of inexplicable frustration.

X

The next evening Mark packed together a few essentials and left Lawborough. He wasn't quite sure of the reasons but after another failed attempt to get the hob working the mountain formed of all his stress and confusion finally collapsed.

The camera had once again turned up nothing, but that was less surprising. Now he knew it had enough mobility to move out of his desk. It didn't seem to follow him in the moment but he now knew it was trying to predict where he was. It wouldn't have manifested in the bin out of randomness, it was trying to place it where he'd see it. So instead of following what he thought was logical he made a snap decision and decided to bail on the whole place. At the very least it might buy him some time he thought.

He didn't officially tell anyone where he was going, he thought it was best to make sure no one knew. Making himself vanish would be surprisingly easy, he already had a reputation for being hard to contact at the best of times so he could easily ignore anyone's attempts. He lived alone, knew no one on the street, and lived in the wrong side of the city for anyone he knew to see him around. Anywhere else he went was irregular enough where they'd take a long time to notice that he hadn't shown his face in a while.

The plan was simple, leave the thing alone. Starve whatever it was of the nourishment it needed to keep writing. A week should be okay, that's all he booked, that's all he's got off work, but he told himself he'll stay more if he doesn't feel confident. After that time return again and pray everything was back to normal. He knew it wasn't the greatest plan in the world, but he knew people in worse positions than him had done better with worse ideas.

He packed a few bare essentials. Clothes, money, phone, laptop, he was scared to bring anything with the potential to write on, like it would have been infected with a thought-based virus.

The nearest hotel he knew was cheap enough to randomly spring a week's stay for one was right on the edge of the city, close enough to the countryside where it was for all intents and purposes out of Lawborough. Somewhat as a joke he was once told that as a strategy running away eventually works and he intended on finally putting it into practice.

He grabbed his singlar bag from his passenger seat and locked his car up in the adjoining lot before eyeing the place up. The hotel managed to be so bland it was gross. The kind of low-effort establishment that looked like what the past thought the present would look like. Everything was clinical whites, blues and yellows, with a plastic sheen over everything from the tables to the doors. There was an attached bar with an overly old-word sign contrasting the whole image, subtly giving away how most of the effort had gone into making it look more effort was put in than was.

"Good evening" the man behind the desk said in the kind of faux-welcoming manner that was typical. The receptionist had a thick accent he couldn't place that made focusing on what he said surprisingly difficult.

"Hi" Mark said, handing him the printed email with confirmation of booking.

"Very good sir. Your room 404. The lift is currently broken so you'll have to climb the stairs"

"Thanks mate"

He took his keycard and receipt and made his way left of the desk to the lift anyway, having completely missed what he was told. He was still tired, very tired, he couldn't remember his last refreshing sleep. The receptionist watched him attempt to call the lift with an indignant look. He tried to play it off as he went for the stairs but had to cross right past the desk to find them.

On his way up he passed a small group of men dressed up in a rainbow pattern of suits. They were tackily bright, each one a parody of a suit and tie in the kind of obnoxious primary colours that seem more fit for a music video from the 80's than a pennies a night hotel. He slid around them as they cascaded down the stairs chanting something that sounded like the kind of inside joke he'd need a decade of context to decipher.

He tried to remember if there were any event on but couldn't pin one down. He'd gotten lost for time the past few weeks and honestly couldn't remember if anything was on the horizon, it could have been Christmas for all he knew, if that weren't implication of something more absurd. All the more justification he needed to feel okay staying put for a few days to reboot.

After climbing the 8 flights of stairs he made it to the 4th floor and made his way to his room. The room had the same watered-down aesthetic that permeated the rest of the hotel, but was at least a modicum more livable than the rest of the hotel. Everything was still in bright colours so getting to sleep would most likely be a pain but there were at least a solidly physical shutter instead of the usual painfully thin blinds.

Unpacking his things he threw them wherever, he wasn't in the right place to sort his clothes into somewhere proper, that could be a job for tomorrow, so let them all sit on the chair for one night. He noticed he'd forgotten to bring any toiletries, again, more to keep him busy over the week. Mark put down his laptop and connected to the wifi. Sifting through the maze of hoops he had to jump through just to access the internet. He didn't intend on going online, as soon as he was done and connected he turned the laptop straight off again. He just wanted to make sure it was doable before he found himself complaining in the morning. Mark turned off his laptop, or rather he tried: it decided it would of all moment like to install updates at that exact time and Mark watched as it struggle to install on the hotel's complimentary wi-fi. That was going to be an all-night job. He buried his laptop under a pile of his clothes to dampen the noise of the fan and put it out of mind.

He turned on the TV and flicked through the channels, eventually landing on an omnibus of old soap operas and let his focus sit on it for the next hour. It was late, and something of no substance that could be chewing-gum for the eyes was exactly what he needed to mellow himself. Tomorrow he would start a new, get up early, go for a run, explore the countryside, and generally unstick himself. By the time he drifted off to sleep, he could still hear his laptop whirring a gentle white noise from beneath the clothes. Just quiet enough to gently lull him to sleep.

XI

<u>Mosyne1995</u> -- New Member -- 2 posts
Posted October 26th 2018 03:10pm
I'm honestly not sure what's going on so I'm just going to say it all. A few days ago I found strange writings appearing in my home without any apparent cause. It's usually the same thing, it's not a direct communication or anything, but I'll go out or simply not be around for a while and I'll come back and more is written. I started it off but it's been a couple of times now where it'll just do its own thing. I've also been able to guide what it's writing by adding my own input (you'll see that on the pictures later) but apart from that and the use of my own name (I'm Mark) it doesn't appear to have anything to do with what I'm saying. I'm about to sink some money into cameras to try and catch something. I've got a scan of some of the stuff <u>here</u> as well as a <u>comparison </u>to my own handwriting (which it doesn't really resemble as you can tell). This has been driving me crazy the past few days and I'm getting nowhere slowly. Does anyone have anything they can say?

Posted October 28th 2018 04:16pm
Sounds really interesting! I'd love to be so close to something like that. Have you tried doing some research into the history of your area? If it is a spirit it's unlikely that it's not stuck around for a purpose and may be limited in its communication. It might be worth looking into the history of your building as well since if I'm following you it doesn't seem to have any mobility beyond where your house. Try contacting the previous owner or Landlord and seeing if any names match up.

<u>Isometries -- Experienced Member -- 263 Posts</u>
Posted October 28th 09:15pm
This seems like a really inefficient way to market your
crappy book guy

CMonexide488 -- New Member -- 1 post
Posted October 30th 03:51am

It seems unlikely anyone can do much to help you now. Often times writing is a reflection of one's own discourse. Is there a lot of emotional energy in your house at the moment? If you don't give yourself proper outlets it can come out in paradoxical ways. I'm not saying it is a reflection of your mental state but what I am saying is you may have a hand in influencing where this is going more than you think. Instead of getting hung up on what's being said try reflecting on what you're doing.

<u>1abugidabby</u> -- <u>Young Member</u> -- <u>85 Posts</u>
Posted October 31st 09:09am
I hate posts like this. Why do the initial talking then not even stick around to do anything. I've searched his name and he's posted this exact message on a couple of other forums and hasn't even acknowledged any of the others yet.

Posted October 31st 2018 11:06pm

There's only one thing sound I can process, and it's not what I can hear. The air is clear and poison permeates it. What gets built will always fall. The sickness is imaginary yet the reality is hurting. The most I can say for her is she gave us one hell of a show. There's only one thing sound I can process, and it's not what I can hear. The air is clear and poison permeates it. What gets built will always fall. The sickness is imaginary yet the reality is hurting. The most I can say for her is she gave us one hell of a show. There's only one thing sound I can process, and it's not what I can hear. The air is clear and poison permeates it. What gets built will always fall. The sickness is imaginary yet the reality is hurting. The most I can say for her is she gave us one hell of a show. There's only one thing sound I can process, and it's not what I can hear. The air is clear and poison permeates it. What gets built will always fall. The sickness is imaginary yet the reality is hurting. The most I can say for her is she gave us one hell of a show. There's only one thing sound I can process, and it's not what I can hear. The air is clear and poison permeates it. What gets built will always fall. The sickness is imaginary yet the reality is hurting. The most I can say for her is she gave us one hell of a show. There's only one thing sound I can process, and it's not what I can hear. The air is clear and poison permeates it. What gets built will always fall. The sickness is imaginary yet the reality is hurting. The most I can say for her is she gave us one hell of a show. There's only one thing sound I can process, and it's not what I can hear. The air is clear and poison permeates it. What gets built.... click to expand

holy_jade -- Admin -- 1301 posts
Posted November 1st 11:21am
Mosyne1995 banned for spam. Thread locked from
further discussion.

XII

Mark walked into the reception late the next morning. He hadn't checked the time but had let himself lay in bed as long as he wanted, hoping it was late enough in the morning that the reception was empty. He still felt awful, and doubted that a night on the cheap hotel mattress had done anything to help.

The reception was completely empty, no one sat behind the counter, he took the first left and looked into the seating area and no one was around, he peeked into the restaurant and there wasn't even someone behind the bar. It gave the place a very barren atmosphere when there wasn't the evermoving people around to distract from the patchy aesthetic. He went to the toothpaste vending machine and checked out the prices. He could see there was one tube left and he put the coins in. Fumbling in the process and dropping a 50p on the floor.

After picking it up and putting it in he put the numbers in and waited for the drop.

The drop never came. He looked up at the machine, it still stonefacedly refused to move. Checking the amount in the machine it hadn't taken the coins, still waiting for a valid input. He looked again at the rack with the toothpaste. It was empty, he could see right to the back of the machine.

Mark ejected his money and pocketed it again. He had no idea what had just happened, whether he'd imagined it or just was too dozy from the morning. He took a right from the desk and made a call for the elevator. After a minute of wasted time he frustratedly conceded that he was an idiot and went left to the stairs. As he opened the door to the stairwell he could tell something wasn't right, something was inexplicably wrong with what he just did, and he couldn't put his finger on what. He stepped back and walked out of the hotel, pricking up his ears. Dead silence in every direction. Not even the rustle of the trees from the breeze he could gently feel beneath his pajamas.

Panicked, he ran down the street to the main road and looked both ways, not a single car was going past either way. There was no way there was no one driving at this time, something was seriously wrong.

He took a few steps backwards and prepared to turn around to return to the hotel. Before he could do so he found himself backed against a wall. He turned to look and saw the front glass wall of the hotel that looked into the lobby. That wasn't right, he'd run for 30 seconds he couldn't have made that distance back already, he turned around again and saw the main road was gone, returned back to its actual position relative to the front doors. He turned around again and made his way inside the hotel, still empty, he made his way to the stairs and began climbing, trying to get back to his room.

He passed floor 1 and looked in, everything looked normal.

He passed floor 2 and looked in, everything looked normal.

He passed floor 3 and looked in, everything looked normal.

He passed floor π and looked in, he stopped, he looked back at the sign, it read 'Floor 2, rooms 201-223'. Mark stood back confused. He turned back down the stairs and after a single set of flights he found himself back in the lobby. He took the first right and sat down in the seating area, still empty.

He took a long, deep, breath, and placed himself in the moment. He was clearly still too sick, needing more time to get it out of his system, he wasn't ready for the outside world again. He tried to listen for anything, any of the ambient noises that comes from being right off a busy street. For a second he heard the sound of a car driving past.

He opened his eyes as it happened, and the floor opened up underneath his seat.

Mark felt the air rushing past his head before he'd begun falling, by the time he'd realised what had happened he'd fell so far down he couldn't see the place he entered from.

Mark took a step forward and found himself back in room 404. Everything was back where it was supposed to be, he had returned. He was still processing everything that had happened so couldn't feel any emotion beneath the intense confusion. He grabbed the nearest thing he could, the kettle, and felt it. It was real, it was definitely there. Mark grabbed the next thing he could, the TV remote, it was also real.

He laughed, a defeated laugh, it was finally over, he thought, time to get back to bed.

As he tried laying down he found that he couldn't. He tried to move himself closer to the bed but from every angle of approach he tried he wasn't getting any closer. The bed wasn't moving, and he was, so everything should've worked but he couldn't get into the bed. He'd lift up the sheets and climb in but still wasn't there, he'd jump on top of it and he'd still not be there, he threw the kettle on the bed, it landed with a soft thump, he tried to pick up the kettle, it was still there.

Making a beeline for the door he opened it and ran into the corridor. Instead of the corridor, he was in his room, the door wrapped back into itself and the same room lie on either side of the door like a freakish reflection. He walked into the mirrored bedroom and tried to get on the bed, it still failed. He walked back into the original room, he couldn't, the door wasn't getting closer as he walked. He could hear a noise coming from the window but was too fearful to investigate.

In a situation of pure terror he was taught you run; if you can't run, you hide; if you can't hide, you fight. As he curled up into a ball on the carpet he realised what you do if you can't fight, you let it get you. He covered his eyes, shutting everything out in the darkness of his hands, and cried.

He could see himself inx the room from above, projected on an ethereal screen above his head. He reeached out to the screen but every movement he made was cancelled out in the other directihon spinning him in place. The screen flickered into life, an old grey film leader counting down from 10. As he thrashed in a vain attempt to escajpe the silent shackles of the void he felt pulses of static through his brain. This place wasn't stable, the fsabric of where he floated was thinly cut, knitted together and didn't need much effort to tear. The screen extended into the infinite in every direction but Mark could see the whole thing as the projeiction crackled and shook as it counted down as Mark tried in vain to reposition himself to hide. Every move he mcadje clouding his surrounding further in meaningless information getdting in the way. He was over a room, like a three dimeensional plan floor plan on a building, he could see into everything. The two actors phased in from somewhere else, somewhere between the room and itself. They were oversimplifications of people, it was hawrd to get a good view, he coujldn't stretch his neck far enough to see tfhe two of them, hed couldn't have been more mmore than a foot away from the screen but he couldn't positiogn himself to see any less than all of it in spmite of his ability to see it. The longer he watched the more he could feel hims grip on the situamtion clouding further, everything he was was blurring in a cacophonous swirl mof flickering light. He reached out to the scene below and stayed firmly rootqed to the void. From his fingers a thick black ink began to seep out, gently leaking in a puddle in all direction. An different black, not the colour black, but leakking from his hand below his head like two liquids blending together was a black borsn from an absence. The absence of cdolour aired all around him as he saw the scene start. The two actors, a Man and a Woman, began, they were virtually indistinguishable and, Mark wasn't sure how he couldd tell which was which. The Man started talking, there was no way for him to be heard by Mark but Mark felt the Man, his body language was uncanny, like a mannequin with extra jointst, whenever Mark jerked his head the room moved to compsensate a second before the actors, the in the space where they moved from it took a second of exposure to the room to return where it should've been behignd the Man, the Man's tone was terriofied, he demonstrated strength anwd fell back on weakness in every word, every word was lost before it came oujt, a movement here, a movement back, the head turned as it spoke, the colourless ink was careful to avoid clouding him. The Woman mmoved identically to the Man, she looked identical, but her tone was different, second-hand, like the Man's but less ernest, there hwas an intangible plasticity to her actions, she too painted anger, but there was no underlying weaknesss, that made her anger echo in the room. One thing came through his head. "It's not supqposed to be like this, you're not supposed to be like this, this isn't how it goes" Like it is came, it left, Mark couldn't remember what he heard. The two continued, back and forth, for a length of time. They occaspionally projected over each other but that awas bad filmmaking so they genuerally let each other finish. Mark couldn't figure out any of it. The Woman would finlish and he would try to reamember any of it but it felt like weeks ago he'd seen it. The Man would finish and he'd remepmber it like it were happeniang presently, Mark rememberued evelry movement of the Man right through tao the end like it had all happened at once. The Woman left the room eventually after countless bounce backs. He saw over thpe doorway, it wpas darker outside, he hadan't noticed the rain, he thought that she should still be inside, once the door closed botuh figures gained a newfound lflexibility, both character changed from oversimplifications to overcomplications, suddeanly Mark could focus on noeither, both became as unseeable as the space between them. pAnother noise caame through his head. It was thue sound of a harpsichord, a single kley, he lcouldn't tell which. The sound was gone, Mark forgot all about it. Both actaors suddenly lost all their character, the veil was stripped, and both stopped projecting whpat thley originally had, instead, they both emitted a dull, quaiet, emotionless, drone, and colluapsed, like the stryinlgs of the puppets had been caut.

The moment the two of them hit the floor the absence ink turned to lightning as it sparked in every direction at an inconceivable speed. Quickly everything Mark could see he couldn't. He could still move, with some effort, like wading through concrete. He tried to see his hands, but all he saw was absence. The only sound was the flutter of the film reel spinning on the projector.

XIII

I don't remember how long had passed between the door slamming shut and a gentle rapping at the door snapping me from my own angst. Maybe only ten seconds and it was Paula turning back to hopefully rope the both of us back in, maybe it was ten hours and it was just the morning postman making the rounds. Either way, I considered how beneficial feigning ignorance would be. Then after a few messages on my phone I'd refused to acknowledge the knocking came back, this time more urgent and deliberate. I separated my eyes from the ceiling fan and looked out the window, it was darker than it had been when she left. The city outside was dead, it was incredibly quiet aside from the mysterious door knocker so he guessed it could only have been around Midnight. I pressed my hands into my eye sockets and pulled them back to see them glistening with a gentle simmer, I hadn't even notice I'd begun to tear up, it had happened so smoothly it felt as natural as breathing. I contemplated the state I'd open the door in, it must have to be Paula, there's no one else it could be at this time, what impression would I give, we'd let ourselves get angered over something and now probably both were in states we regretted. Maybe it'd be better if I let myself look in a state, a visual apology before any actual words.

Paula wasn't at the door, I figured that out as I undid the lock, considering why it was even locked, she must've taken a key to lock it from the outside after all. After giving the key the final turn I hurriedly considered who it could be before the door began to push itself open and a familiar, petite figure emerged from around it, I recognised her instantly but the name took a second to come to me, not until she lowered her hood and turned to face me.

Ella.

"Ella?"

Ella pulled her wet hair back into a ponytail and hooked her coat up. Giving me a crooked smile that entailed a dozen emotions, primarily: the smile of mischief. Before I could begin another question she pressed her body against mine and her lips met mine with a harsh force. Pushing me back in the process all the way into the main room and down onto the sofa where she sat on top of me. All the while letting her rich maroon lipstick stain every ridge around my mouth. I was so caught up in the animalistic rush of euphoria that such a passionate kiss releases it wasn't until she stopped and began to run her nails against my chest that I was able to process anything apart from her.

"Listen Mark, I know what just happened"

I desperately stammered for anything to say but came up with nothing.

She laughed at my confusion and wrapped herself around my shoulders before continuing "She went to Alex's after you fought, I was there, she told us everything. I made my excuses and came here. I know how you're feeling right now Mark, go with it"

I felt her pull me in again and she grabbed my hands, guiding them to her hips as she began spreading her lipstick onto my neck. I tensed up as I felt her acquaint herself with the shape of my sides and back and she pushed herself back again.
"Sometimes you just need to get it out of you, a purge of your bad juju is the best medicine for any ailment, sometimes when I get sick of Alex I find a guy for a hard night to get it out, you should do the same"

She gave me another forceful kiss and stood. Bending over while unbuttoning her top to whisper into my ear "Here's what I'm going to do, I'm going to go upstairs and find your bedroom, I'm going to close the door and get out of these clothes, if after 5 minutes you're not knocking on the door I'll get the message and leave. Not a word will be spoken thereafter, it'll be like this never happened. It's your choice Mark"

She finished and turned around, letting her shirt fall to the floor exposing the silky smooth back and the lines of a navy blue brazier. Before I could even fathom another word she was gone and the sound of a bedroom door gently closing came from above. I wiped my mouth, then my shoulder, and pulled back half a dozen stains of reddish-brown. I tried to stand but my head was spinning harder than anything a night of liquor had done to me since sixth form. I stumbled back and lent against the doorframe, staring at the stairs and began seriously considering the next four minutes. That four minutes turned to three before he'd even constructed a coherent line of thought.

Then the three fell to two.

I'd swear it were out of my control, I truly did feel like my legs were moving on their own but I knew there was some core fault of my persons that lead me up to Ella. I ran around her words "a purge of your bad juju is the best medicine for any ailment", even if it was one of the worst ways to say it, she'd captured something raw in the words she chose. It was enough to capture him, ensnare him for the night. I gently tapped on the door and heard a coy cooing from the other side. Quietly hoping she'd vanished I scanned the room but found her with a hideslick grin sitting at my desk, flicking through a random notebook. Now bearing her form only with a few scant pieces of lingerie and a cigarette between two fingers. She got up and pulled me in again, this time I could feel her soft skin, fire to the touch. I felt her hourglass physique as I pulled apart my shirt, traced my fingers around her lotus-flower tattoo on her shoulder blade as she took off my belt, and as we both ran out of clothes to remove I gazed upon her body as a whole as I laid back in my bed. I took the sight in, every taper, every curve, every cold point and warm edge. I gazed long into her, and she gazed back.

Mark finished writing, he dotted the final sentence with a sealing lock and dropped his pen. He couldn't remember when he'd stopped reading what was already there and began to continue, maybe he just wrote the whole thing there and then, deluded himself into thinking that whatever power had been haunting him had decided to be so cruel and put himself through it. He couldn't even remember when he'd returned back home.

But as he stared down at the wreaths of papers on his desk he stepped back and took a deep breath. He swore for just a moment he could smell the smoke from Ella's cigarette and could see her again betwixt his bedsheets.

Mark climbed in the shower and gave himself a blast of the coldest it could go, he felt filthy, like he'd truly done something to hurt someone, Paula. The image of Ella climbing on top of him couldn't leave his head no matter how hard he tried. He sat down, still under the showerhead and realised he was still in his clothes, now darkened by the freezing water trickling down his face pretending to hide the leaking from his eyes. He spent the rest of the day sitting there. Letting the emotions get out of his system, thoroughly wasting water, and letting the details of the scene leak away and spiral down the drain.

It was afternoon by the time he left the shower, feeling numb and cold from the water. Mark took off and squeezed out his clothes before leaving them on a radiator to dry. He got into a new outfit and walked back to his desk. Gathering up the night, he tucked it away in the Graveyard drawer, where the rest of his time with Paula had been tucked in. From his basement he got together a stack of newspapers from the burn pile and brought them to his kitchen, splaying them out over the countertop as he began preparing some dinner. He looked through the articles he'd written in the past and spent the rest of the day remembering what it was like when he didn't care about the things he wrote.

XIV

The next morning Mark woke up with an atrocious feeling of unrest in his stomach; draped in a batch of old newspapers and half his bedsheets. He tried desperately to think of where he had to be that day but could only draw to mind the vivid memory of his own fiction. A growl of his stomach made him wonder of the last time since returning back to Lawborough that he'd eaten anything more than snack food and takeaways. It was his body's demand for something that wasn't crawling in salt and preservatives that he pulled him out of bed in the end as it threatened to churn out what little was in it. He reached for his bedside tissues but the box was empty and knew he probably didn't have any replacements around.

After taking the last of the roll from the bathroom for clearing out his throat and folding up his dried clothes from the previous afternoon he made his way downstairs. More old newspapers lay across most of the surfaces in the kitchen and living room but apart from that the house was surprisingly habitable, he pressed his mind for answers and could return vague outlines of himself putting things away after his episode. He fished through cabinets and pulled together the stuff for an old school fryup like he knew from University but tried for the gas to find it still out. He tried to laugh at his ineffectual landlord but was unable through a cloud of phlegm so he silently put away the ingredients before sifting through the piles of teetering-on-the-edge-of-off ingredients and settling down on his couch with a sandwich. Letting the mundanity of his 7am breakfast wake him up as he figured out what he was supposed to do with his day to get him away from his desk.

His answer came not much longer after he'd finished. An unprovoked phone call from Hayley that he leapt at to answer.

"Hello Hayley"

"Mark?" She, in spite of being the one who called him, seemed surprised to hear his voice.

"Yes…"

"Oh, sorry, I've been called in by Rose today to talk about my interning so I really can't cover for you today"

The back of Mark's throat grew rough again, partly in guilt of the knowledge that even not counting his scheduled time away he'd not done any proper work in at least a week.

He took so long to return she awkwardly continued "... and your buffer's run out too, you really need to come back to work today"

Mark stumbled "Yeah okay, is there a specific thing they want me to go to or is it just logistical stuff today"

"I'll text you the details, they want someone at a school thing today"

"Thanks Hayley" I prepared to hang up and start getting ready before I heard more from her.

"Hey Mark?"

"Yes?"

She hesitated a few seconds as I sat there waiting "Did your time away do you any better?" she asked, sounding heartwarmingly genuine "Just I and the rest of the place has been worried for you"

He let out a single laugh before sputtering like an old outboard motor "Still feeling like shit but a functional shit is at least better than idle shit"

"That's good to hear I guess?"

"Yes it is, now if you'll excuse me I need to actually start getting ready, you'll message me the details"

"Yeah, bye Mark".

He put his phone to one side and began getting ready. Picking up a paper from the arm of the seat on the way and setting the kettle to boil. As it did he flicked through the paper for his own section in the central third. The front page was about parliamentary expenses so he could recall exactly what he was looking for in that issue, an interview with a duckhouse maker as a throwback to the last time it happened. But as he flicked through he stopped to look at an article about a couple of now irrelevant celebrities getting divorced and took note of an oddity.

Their faces had been cut out, as well as the right edge of the first paragraph and the bottom half of the headline, a neat square of missing paper. He poked his finger through to confirm the obvious and turned over the page to see what else was missing. The rectangle perfectly took out a single article besides another banal piece. The space usually reserved for an article just like the one he was looking for.

He dropped the paper and reached for another, one that was resting in the thankfully dry sink. Flicking through it again he searched for his own article, this was a recent enough paper where he could vaguely recall it being about hoodlums making rude graffiti in a nearby park but the paper had the same problem. This time an L-shaped hole that took out half an advertisement for cosmetics along with it. A third paper gave the same result, a rectangular hole. After the fourth he'd gotten the message and took a step out into the hallway. He ran upstairs and back to his desk to check his writings, it ended in the same place as it did last night. He went back downstairs and closed both the kitchen and living room doors, secretly hoping putting a physical barrier between himself and the mystery would speed up in making him forget about it.

"No, not dealing with this anymore, fuck you, I'm not biting" he said, to no one in particular.

Hayley's text came in as he got dressed in his final ironed shirt. 'Sherston Primary off Mill Road are crowning a goat a teacher at twenty past 9. Forgot the reason why but you're the pro here find that out yourself. Prolls just talk to a teacher and a few of the kids oki?'

Mark replied 'Have I been gone so long 'prolls' is an acceptable thing to say?' and 'I'll prolls be fine'

Mark arrived at Sherston around 9:10 and found a very slapdash fence in the front yard being watched intently by a walking stereotype in a green jacket and flatcap to hold a very disgruntled looking goat. Both of which were being overlooked by a similarly disgruntled looking woman desperately sucking on a cigarette to keep herself warm. Mark assumed she was a teacher who'd drawn the short straw of being the one to overlook the goat and his owner while the children were doing whatever schools do in the morning now.

He picked up his Lawborough Press-marked notepad from the glove compartment and walked up to the trio. Exchanging the polite nods of acknowledgement with the goat and its owner before attracting the woman's attention. She seemed on the older end of teachers, probably in her 50's and a distinct clouding in her right eye that only added to her already glazed staring off into the middle-distance. I introduced myself and she looked to be manually focusing on my name badge.

"So you're the wally they got in" she had a rough voice from years of chainsmoking that added an unwelcoming air to her expressionless face. "This ain't my first dumb stunt so here's the situation"

Mark began to write, flowering it up the whole time

"The head had this particular killer idea, all this alternative learning shit we're being told to do has lead to this"

'Alternative learning is giving our kids all kinds of opportunities'

"So instead of proper science like I wanted to do, they all got to play with this dumb goat instead"

'A hands-on exploration of biology'

"Because they'll always need to know where their lambchops are coming from rather than multiplication tables"

'Alternative learning helps give students a look at the world outside of the classroom'

"Not all bad, my uncle..." the man grunted behind her "...manages to get a little bit of cash out of it and I'm getting a cut"

'Resourceful teachers'

"And it went down so well the head even drew up a fake employment contract we're going to get the goat to sign"

'They thanked their wollen companion with its own job!'

Mark sniggered "Didn't know the job market was that easy at the moment"

The teacher took another drag and stubbed it out on the floor.

"Nice to see I'm not alone in seeing how dumb this is"

"It could be worse, they'll have plenty of time to learn about their 6's and 7's" Mark responded, playing devil's advocate.

"I'm sure when all these kids are on their way to Oxbridge they'll be so influenced by this dumb stunt"

"That seems a bit of a pessimistic way of looking at it"

The school bell rang and a spontaneous landslide of kids emerged from the school in what flustered looking teachers were attempting to turn into coherent lines. The woman turned to look away and pulled an envelope from her pocket before ending the conversation.

"Gimmicks don't lead to enlightenment, proper education does, I thought someone stuck reporting this bollocks would understand that" She turned to walk towards a particular group and Mark was left awkwardly standing around waiting for someone to tell him what to do next.

Mark circled around the fence again and took in the sight of the students, looking for someone in a position of even minor authority to make him look like something other than an anonymous adult floating around a sea of children. Fortunately most of the children were too distracted in their momentary fancies to care and the grownups were either tangled up in other work or exhausted from the effort to care. He eventually zoned in on a balding man with wireframe glasses and a tie, taking him as the most professional looking person of the lot.

"Hi, I'm with the paper?" He asked before realising it wasn't technically a question.

The man turned around and gave him a quick run down before pointing him towards another with an atonal "you want him"

The process repeated itself another time before Mark found himself tapping on the shoulder of a Hawaiian shirt talking to a group of older looking students. The man turned around and immediately pushed Mark back with an uncomfortable wave of optimistic energy. He was trying far too hard to be cool.

"You're the one from the Press! I thought they were sending a woman over"

"Um, no, she got, caught up in something. I'm Mark Bishop" He said reaching his hand for a shake that lasted an uncomfortably long time.

"Glad you came, I'm Gerry. I'm hoping you can help me the voice that takes the power of making education fun to the masses."

Mark rolled his mental eyes at the thought "Yes well it is certainly unique..."

Before Mark could finish his pause for breath Gerry continued "I've been in this job for a few licks short of a decade now and have never lost that spark of passion for filling the children with an awe for education. Every day is a front-line assault on the boring stereotype of fractions and rhyme schemes and I trust you're getting all this?"

"Oh I certainly am" Mark said, finishing off tracing the same circle to a point where it was burnt in the page below. "How are you getting the goat to sign the contract? It's probably just going to eat it."

"Exactly!"

"Okay..."

Mark scribbled down a quick 'Headstrong Headmaster' and moved on to get a better view of the proceedings.

"Now Children I know you've all enjoyed your time with our Goaty friend, but unfortunately his time with us is over"

The children all aww'd on cue and the second the noise began they took it as a sign to get distracted and start their own conversations. Multiple teachers had to fumble to get them to quieten down so Gerry could continue.

"Now, don't be sad, we must remember that she'll never truly be gone so long as we remember him. Remember her, and he'll be in your heart...

The chainsmoker teacher from earlier leant over "He talks like they're in Nursery"

"Nursery kids he doesn't have much confidence in" he remarked.

"...and you Harry, you'll remember the time we all visiter her on the farm. And you Julie, you'll remember when he and us..."

Mark leaned in "Why does he keep swapping between genders?"

A different teacher leant in from behind to answer, his breath stank of garlic "Apparently it's to make it more inclusive"

"But surely that makes no sense, pick one, pick neither, pick something, swapping randomly confuses everyone"

"You're telling me - heads up lad"

"...you're still sad after all that. We are here to present him with this degree of education from us. So she'll be welcome to come and visit us here at Sherston any time!" the crowd of children all cheered as he leant in with the scroll of paper. Clearly posing for a camera that Mark suddenly remembered that he had left in the boot of his car. Gerry stood awkwardly over the pen with the paper for several seconds before he accepted that Mark hadn't even tried to capture the moment and dropped it in.

As expected, the goat ate it.

The children didn't seem to care though, an uproar of cheers and laughing came from the crowd as they lapped up the whole process.

"Now it's time for you all to get back to lessons" Gerry interrupted, demonstrating impressively little crowd control, since they were perfectly happy to completely ignore him. "You'll get to see her again during break!"

After a few minutes of what Mark could only assume was watching Gerry squirm the teachers began helping and managed to herd the children inside leaving Mark, Gerry, the flatcap and the Goat. Mark decided the Goat was the most tolerable company in the yard and went to fetch his camera from the back of his car. It had been jostled behind a plastic bag that had been in his boot so long he'd forgotten what was in it. When he returned he found Gerry talking at a the stereotype, absolutely refusing to budge a single facial muscle in response.

"Ah yes, Matt was it? Anyway I trust seeing this you'll do a fine job of being a key part in the expansion of my philosophy. And I'm sure you'll thank old Paul A. here"

"I'm sorry, what was his name?"

"Paul. We have another Paul on staff here so we used his other initial to split them" Paul grunted, either in disgust or acknowledgement.

Mark turned around "No, no, not biting" he said, pointing angrily at the sky "you can try all you want, I'm fucking done"

"What?" Gerry said, clearly not totally registering what he'd heard.

"Nothing"

Mark leant down to eye up the shot. Debating what would look least terrible with the least amount of effort.

"What's its name?" he asked,

"The school elected a neutral name, we called her Alex" Gerry gormlessly declared like he was wallowing in victory

"Oh course it is, why should I have expected otherwise, nice one"

Gerry looked at Mark, not entirely sure how he was expected to respond to a remark clearly not made at him yet with no one else it could have been.

"I'm serious, stop it" Mark muttered under his breath as he lined up the photograph to get the school in the background.

He made his excuses at that point and decided to go, whatever this place was it was seemingly barreling down on him to stop ignoring the impossible and he needed to get out of there. For general politeness he tried to avoid looking like he was making a mad break but couldn't imagine a way he was successful.

As he opened the boot of his car he noticed again the tied up bag in the corner. It seemed to had moved to the other corner of the boot since he'd collected his camera. He carefully placed it down and reached for the bag, trying to remember what it was and how long it had been there. It had been so long ago that he just never remembered a time where it wasn't there. Maybe something to do with safety? Always having a supply kit in case of emergency? Something like that. It was tied around the top low enough where he couldn't see inside at all.

An assault of scraps of paper sprung out of the bag when he tore it open. They erupted with enough kinetic energy to throw him off-balance. The bag was deceptively densely packed and hundreds of hand-sized pieces exploded across is boot and out into the world. The breeze immediately sent a few dozen most energetic ones out into the street like a ticker-tape parade. Mark clambered to close the boot and thankfully the flurry had managed to avoid attracting attention. The clips were all small enough for some to be invisible to the eye already and he watched the rest drift away in a dance of black-on-white.

In his stumble for balance, he had managed to successfully stand on a couple of pieces however. Briefly considering the possibility of quashing his curiosity by kicking them away he picked them up anyway and read. The first of the two was an article, a familiar article, with the headline "Pie Sent Into Stratosphere For Scientific Research", the second, equally familiar "World Record For Knitting Set By Lawborough Grandma" both proudly signed by Mark Bishop.

Mark went flush.

XV

As reality began to trickle back into Mark he could taste the inexplicable taste of sawdust. It was the kind of complete oddity of flavor that he was able to focus in on it. Grounding himself in the moment he washed the sawdust around his mouth before spitting it out. He looked up and saw it had turned to night since he last remembered. It was dark, very dark. He tried to stand back up but couldn't quite coordinate himself well enough to do so, so he remained laying down, groggily trying to get the sawdust out of his mouth.

He tried again to stand up, reaching against a nearby wall to force himself up but only ended up pressing his hand against unexpected corners and barriers that he couldn't quite comprehend as well as he could taste the grains. He tried bending his knees but every time he hit them against a solid surface with a slight bit of buckle to it. He tried rolling over but without light he couldn't comprehend exactly what he was trying to do and ended up the same way he started.

Holding his eyes open he tried to focus on the sky. Seeking out the clouds or the stars but all he saw was darkness.

As he began to feel around himself he pieced where he was together: he wasn't outside, it wasn't night time, he was inside of something. He'd begun to regain his ability to control his actions and press9%ed upwards. Unable to completely extend his arms before being met with resistance, he had to be laying in a space at most two foot deep. He tried pressing outwards instead and was met with the realisation of how claustrophobic the space he was laying was. A wooden space a few inches deeper, a few inches wider, a few inches longer than he was.

Mark tried to panic and hit the side he was facing as hard as he could, the wooden surface flexed slightly but remained resilient. A second attempt left his hand hurting too much to think about trying again so he swapped hands and threw another punch at the darkness. He recoiled from the pain of the third attempt and clasped his hands together, feeling a few warm droplets flowing from a cut in the palm of his hand that seemed too fine to be from the wall. He pressed his ear to the side and tapped, hearing echoless thumbs that indicated a solid other side.

Mark took a deep breath to quash his fear and after a few dozen more he gathered himself together enough to systematically search the area. The room wasn't a perfect shape, it tapered off above his head to a point like it had a corner cut from the edge of it and the surface to his left was smooth as stone as opposed to the others that were all wooden. What felt like the traces of a latch or handle with no grip was on the surface above him with hinges against it.

He tried again to push but he felt too weak from waking up suddenly and his general poor health to counter the considerable force keeping it in place. He let himself flop back down and tried desperately to recall how he got there but whenever he thought past the schoolyard the sick feeling in the pit of his stomach bubbled up and caused him to lose focus.

He felt his surroundings again, making sure there was no detail left unchecked. After confirming there was nothing else he could attempt apart from having another go at the front he turned focus to himself.

Dipping into his pockets he pulled out his phone; temporarily blinding himself with the brightness of the screen. He noted the time and the battery and that both were worryingly in the small numbers: 8:06am Thursday, only nine percent battery left. Acting quick he navigated to the keypad and entered 999 then sat waiting for a response.

Three long tones, then silence.

Mark looked down, his phone had no signal; he double checked in the settings and saw nothing. The phone battery ticked down another percent.He let out a cry of frustration and dropped his phone in the process. He swore a few times and picked it back up before switching on th8%e phone's torch to get another look at where he was. The inspection confirmed everything he'd already figured out. He was laying down in a small wooden room with a single hatch that covered most of the part he was facing. The tiny area illuminated by the flashlight made it hard to get a full picture, yet still a sense of deja vu came over him as he combed the area: not exactly sure what he was looking for.

Mark turned the light onto himself, struggling to get a good look at what he was wearing thanks to the restricted space. He was in the same shirt he wore the previous day, but had different scruffier trousers and his shoes were missing. His hands were a bloodshot red from hitting the walls and the insides of his palms were covered in cuts marks like they'd grabbed a fistful of stinging nettles; a few were fresh enough where they still left smudges of blood when rubbed over.

After another failed attempt to brute force the door down he returned to the phone and began desperately searching through his apps. They looked weird for some reason and he couldn't put his finger on why. Without a connection to the outside world he was unable to get more than a few seconds deep into most of the ones he wanted before it spat in his face an error or unpassable loading screen. Heavily breathing the whole time he opened his messenger and looked through the last received messages hoping that whatever had been done to him was done by someone polite enough to contact him through social media beforehand.

The app took its time opening as to milled over the lack of connection but eventually let him in, presenting him with his recent contacts. His messenger was mostly old news but sitting perched atop the list of recent contacts was the highlighted picture of Jason Now7%ak, indicating an unopened message, a message said to have been received at 19:39 on Wednesday according to the app, a day mark couldn't recall when exactly it was in relation to now.

[18:40] Hey you alright man?
[18:41] I saw that thing you posted.
    I'm fine man, just got a lot going on right about now [19:03]

[19:05] Is this about that girl you been seeing?

Kinda, things are strange [19:07]

[19:08] Dude, your post was a cry for attention you can't pretend like you're not going to talk it when someone gives in

It's not as simple as you think [19:11]

Wait, what thing I posted? I've not posted anything [19:11]

What the fuck I didn't post that [19:12]

[19:14] That makes no sense. You acknowledged it.

I've been fluey all week so I didn't process it. [19:15]

[19:16] Didn't process what?

I swear to god I didn't do this [19:16]

That's so not good. I've got no clue what's going on [19:17]

[19:19] "I've got no clue what's going on" is the exact wording you used in the post.

How did you know that I deleted the post [19:20]

You wrote it didn't you, it's you trying to fuck with me [19:21]

Fucks sake man you've got no clue what this is doing [19:21]

Things aren't cool right now don't do that shit [19:21]

[19:23] I wrote it, or I just still had the page open.

Sure whatever. Either way ignore it [19:25]

[19:27] Whatever man, do whatever. I tried indulging you and all you're doing is writing me shit. Have fun in your little world.

No dude, I'm sorry. It's just complicated right now [19:28]

[19:39] When people say that most of the time it's you causing the problem.

The messages ended there. The beginnings of a response Mark had written was sitting at the bottom of the page, unsent at the time yet kept in the window awaiting the request to be sent.

This is all just as fake as my problems, I swear [Send]

After a double check of the rest of the conversations he could find for any other unsent messages he closed the phone. Trying to recall having that conversation. He constructed the image of himself, sitting somewhere, probably at his office chair, typing away at Jason desper6%ately trying to make sense of the information he was then processing and now re-processing but couldn't construct more than an dramatic recreation of how he imagined it went down, an amalgamation of other times he'd done similar things attempting to pass as a new thought. He thought about how he'd heard it was impossible to remember something for the first time, and desperately fought against the conclusion that it was lost for good.

In vain Mark tried sending the final message but it was shunted back down and returned another error message.

After closing the messenger and brushing more sawdust off of his body he locked the phone and let the darkness of his surroundings enter him again.

He could hear nothing, he could see nothing, there was no smell in the air and no ambient rumbles from anywhere nearby. The sensory deprivation was a kind that he'd never experienced before. He turned his phone back on to burn a hole in the dark and looked at his home screen.

Suddenly it came to him, why all of a sudden his phone looked so strange. Most of the time he had the phonebook in the bottom corner, closest to his thumb, for ease of access. But it'd been moved, instead his notepad app was in the bottom corner; inconspicuously sitting there like it had the right to do so. After loading the app he noted another change.

It was empty. Every note he'd ever taken on his phone had been replaced with empty pages. From the recent takes on work and websites to his ancient reminders of family birthdays. It was all gone. There must've been dozens he'd made over time and never got around to cleaning out. All gone.

Except for one note, untitled.

Mark knew exactly what it was when he saw it.

The worst thing, the thing that stuck to my mind so much harder than anything else, was when Ella left. When we were done, she was still confident, like nothing had happened.

"I like a keepsake" she said, almost reveling in my inability to match her satisfaction. She looked on my desk and out a book from the pile I like to keep close to hand, a book called Every Day. "I saw this when waiting for you, I read this a few years ago, lost my copy, mind?"

I knew it'd get her out quicker if I let her. Her smile wasn't as warm as Paula's, it was a rougher, tricker smile. A prankster's smile. She got the5% rest of her clothes on in a flash and before I could think long enough to find my jeans her outfit was back in one piece. "You've got my number, I'm always down"

After what we did I didn't sleep in the bed, I'm not sure I could have brought myself to do it without being forced to think about it any more than I already had. I wanted to get myself as far away from it as possible.

I got my shirt and trousers on and watched her leave out the bedroom window. I imagined her going back to Alex, that's probably not where she went, but I imagined her going back and acting like nothing happened. Imagining how on earth she was capable of keeping different people in the dark. Maybe that's why she wasn't talkative, always trying to keep the right people in the right amount of dark so she could tell any story. I admired it, to an extent, the same extend I was disgusted by it.

I let the night air into my room and only as I took a deep breath did I realise how tired I'd gotten. I was shattered. It was already late when I'd yelled at Paula, it must've been hours ago now, the light was going to break soon and I'd done nothing but burn energy for the past quarter of a day.

Every attempt to distract myself enough to escape what I did ended in vain. I'd push something to the front of my mind and I'd always spiral back on it. It was inescapable. I didn't want to think about it but I think something inside of me knew what I wanted wasn't what I needed.

I looked at the stubbed out cigarette Ella had left on my desk, my own keepsake of what I did, the ashes staining the finely polished wood. I moved my phone over it to try and hide the burn but in doing so I unlocked it. I had three unread messages. All from hours ago, all of which were from Ella, of course they were.

I felt flush, as I opened the mess4%ages. I didn't read them, I just wanted them gone from my notifications. My face began to burn under the guilt. I'd done it, I'd really done it, I'd let myself crumble under the promise of release and had fucked up badly. My head felt heavy, it felt like all the blood in my body has pumping through my face trying to drown my own thoughts. My pulse slowed to a crawl but every pump was like a shotgun blast in my head. I felt it between my eyes and right in the back of my skull. Every throb I felt like I deserved, and as I put my head between my hands I desperately scrunched up to try and stop it.

I could barely string together a thought, the sudden rush of blood through my system completely threw me off. I tried to stand and put myself closer to the cool air of the outside and collapsed onto the window frame, dragging across the glass as I went to the floor. My head landed directly on the corner of the chair and knocked me to the side. I wasn't knocked out, fortunately it only dazed me for a few seconds. I felt my face for blood and came back dry.

I tried to stand back up again, this time carefully taking each action. It wasn't too bad, just needed to focus. I got onto my hands and knees and took a pause for breath. My house keys were on the floor, probably fell out of m3%y pocket. Oh god no don't think about that, I pass on them, throwing them into a corner somewhere to be found later. I stood back up, let myself mentally stabilize and looked around. Everything was fine. I just need to not think too hard. The cocktail of stress and emotion was deadly when consumed too much.

I picked up my car keys. I knew I needed to find Paula, I needed to apologise,tell her everything say I did it out of weakness, I know I'm not owed her, but I want to do it for myself. It wasn't in the first draw I checked, second draw contained a pack of mints I'd forgotten I had, they'd be good, clear my head, I picked a couple out and threw them in, third draw had the keys.

I threw on my shoes without even socks and ran for the car. Nearly falling on the door as I fumbled with the buttons to unlock it. I looked around, it was early, I think, it was late enough in the morning where I could make out the shapes of the street without the effort but everything was still mostly black, grey, blues and a few bright yellow lights through windows that were obviously artificially bright.

I stalled the car. Dumbass. Good job.

"You're..." I tried talking to myself, then realised that was weird, then realised that I knew no one was around so didn't need to care about looking weird, then I realised how weird thinking this hard about it was. I'm fine either way, which was the point. I start driving.

I pull out and begin trying to remember where she lived. It was basically diagonal through most of the suburbs. That was a lot of finicky corners and one-ways between us that even I could tell I w2%asn't able to do sober. I'm fine to get there, just need to head the long way, through some of the dual carriageways and the busier streets. Shouldn't be busy, nothing's looking busy as I make my way off the sidestreets and pull on to Bluebrook Road. There's no one else anywhere. Apart from that one car going the other way. I try to remain unremarkable and not-in-a-hurry for as long as it remains in my rearview mirror and as soon as it's gone I return to the task at hand.

I keep going. I saw a green light go red, can't've been more than a few hundred yards away. How fast was I going? I saw a thing once that stuff looks greener if you're going fast. Something like that anyway. There was no way that was true for people though. The light stayed red I think, don't know, didn't see it shortly after either way. Might've been a different light anyway, intersections have a lot of lights. No other cars are going my way so I'll be okay. There's a horn, I think it's my own, either way I can't hear it anymore already. It's hard to keep *hold of the wheel properly when you're trying to dry your own eyes so I probably hit the horn.*

The next light is just yellow by itself when I see it. Shit does that mean it's about to go Red or Green? It's fifty-fifty, plenty of safe things can happe1%n if I go for it. I go for it. There's a noise, like the noise of a can being stood on, the wheel's started to turn itself. I think anyway, it's getting away from me again. The back corner of the car gets thrown out of line and it's took the rest of the car with it. I'm in the car still, of course, so I'm taken as well.

The sound of the tires hitting the curb made a noise I can't even fathom. It was all quieter than I imagined it would be though. It was a tall curb I drifted into, it shunted the whole car forward, I think, I've lost track of what exactly is going on. I was being blinded by a lamppost, why the hell were they still on I can see fine, I was off the driver's seat now facing up through the sunroof, forgot to buckle up, I crawled back up and tried to get my hands on the wheel but all I grabbed was the dashboard that had flung itself open b0%

The screen went black. A second passed. Mark dropped his phone. Darkness prevailed again throughout the room. The impenetrable darkness caked everything around him in mystery.

The silence got to him most that time, the ear-splitting silence of absolute, unfiltered nothing rang hollow in his ears. Every slightest shuffle of his person or creak against the wooden floor felt cacophonous compared to the silence. Every noise he made got swallowed in it, a spark of stimulation fed to the insatiable silence.

The darkness began to move under his feet as his panic clawed its way in.

It was a tiny trickle of movement at first, but Mark saw it immediatly, the darkness was moving, replacing and reshifting itself around him. Nothing was moving, however, he would try to position himself to stamp out or grab the movement and he'd always hit the walls half an inch before he could interact with anything. Without the frames of reference he couldn't see that any movements were beyond his box. Sitting meters away when he knew he couldn't take a step towards them.

He closed his eyes but only saw the same. The dark ebbing over the middle-distance and encircling him. He blinked rapidly. Trying to flutter them away but both states became indistinguishable where he'd forget if he'd left his eyes open or closed when focusing on them. The dark was there, it was invisible, wrapped in the blackness and indistinguishable from anything else, but what was moving was there. He could tell what it was, he watched it move, saw what shape was circling him. He felt ever curve of it, felt every detail of it. He recognised the features and couldn't explain what he saw. He saw nothing.

Mark began again to push, he pushed forwards as hard as he could again, then to the sides, then underneath him, then up and down, then forwards again, he felt the wood underneath his palms squeeze slightly under his force, he kept pushing, trying to follow. Every muscle in his arms screamed as he desperately clung on to anything he could. The maelstrom of darks infesting his vision formed around him. She had moved further back again, threatening to go out over the horizon of the dark and to leave him alone again with the rough seas but he continued. He lifted his legs up and positioned himself seated and pushed up with them instead. He heard a crack, a creak, then a passing truck rumbled the room, then another crack, the truck reinvigorated him, the first noise he'd heard that wasn't his own, another crack, something buckled under his force, how did he hear a truck, something loud snapped, the roof gave way.

Before Mark knew it he fell, as the hatch opened and the light of the outside world returned to his he felt himself falling. He landed bottom first and pressed his back against the wall for stability.

As his eyes panicked to adjust he dragged himself up and focused on where he was. The room was now exposed to the light and he could see everything, three wooden walls, a roof that tapered into one edge, a stone wall to the other side, a smooth wooden floor.

He turned around again and looked around his hallway. He looked at the pale blue walls, he looked down the hall to his front door and saw the bin lorry's flashing lights breaking through the glass. He turned around and looked into his kitchen, every surface buried under reams of old newspapers

Mark picked up his phone and closed his under-stair cupboard door.

XVI

It was like something he'd've read when he was a teenager, Mark thought. The tale of a man driven insane by a mechanical oracle. Sick of working with screwdrivers and pencils resorting to more blunt instruments. In the late of the following night night Mark grabbed his own toolkit and an empty milk jug and took a step back from his house. He wasn't wearing and socks or shoes and could feel the fine cracks of the road under his toes. He stepped back further and further until he'd crossed the road and he backed into the house parallel his own. The whole time not breaking eye contact with his bedroom window, looking for a break, some sign of another thinking being trying to call his bluff but all he could see was the reflection of the sky off of the glass.

He walked back to his side of the street and got in his car. Every action was calculated and deliberate, intentionally exaggerating his movements to a point where any casual observer could easily make out what he was doing; but the humdrum residential streets in the middle of the night attracted no traffic beyond the stars: and they were thoroughly uninterested in him. Mark popped the bonnet of the car and got out to inspect. He tried to make out the details under the streetlight but struggled to parse the shadows from the rust and pulled out his own torch.

He knew a fair amount about the mechanics of the car from television but it was a online tutorial of engine deconstruction that he was thinking of as he reached in with a pair of pliers. Fishing his way through each element of the machine like a pig sniffing for truffles. After a second attempt with his torch in his mouth he managed to locate the line he was looking for and gently grabbed it with the pliers enough not to puncture. He grabbed the jug and carefully navigated it through the engine to underneath to catch the consequences of the cut.

Mark cut the line and let the petrol gently drain. It poured out fast enough to fill the half-litre container before Mark could parse what he was doing and the rest overflew and dripped onto the road below. Mark lay on the side of the car for a moment. Watching the fuel drop through the rest of the engine and onto the road surface, slowly making its own way toward a nearby drain and to who-knows from there. He thought of how much he'd left in the tank but was numb to the numbers of liters he'd be wasting.

Leaning back up Mark pressed the bonnet back down and waited to hear the click before taking back his keys and picking up his jug. He remained deliberate, making sure to hold it in the hand that gave the bedroom window the best view of the petrol.

The house remained unflinching.

Mark left the front door unlocked and placed the container by the top of the basement stairs. He felt like he should be doing something more fitting of the situation as he made his way to upstairs and into his bedroom. The expectation was always for a dramatic internal monologue before an action of great importance but Mark remained businesslike in his actions. Only thinking to himself exactly what he was doing in the moment. Open the door, gently, grab the notebooks, checking for loose papers or anything else with Paula's name, a nick of cheap poundland cider, still cold from the fridge, close the door. He thought himself an artisan, carefully crafting his actions to make the product as pristine as possible. After grabbing everything he could he returned to his basement. Leaving the light off resulting in the only illumination being from the hallway and a faint glow of moonlight from a surface-level window. Mark broke his own facade and wondered how long that window had been left open before snapping back as he reached the bottom of the stairs.

After working out roughly where the centre of the room was he pulled up an old box of miscellaneous and placed his collection on it. Like an offering to an ancient god he made sure they were pristine, in line with the edges of the cardboard and in as fine a condition as they could be. He gently dusted them off and made sure a page was exposed.

"Your move" he said out loud to the air. He noted a gentle cold breeze come in from the window which he knew was worthy of ignoring but he made sure to wait until it stopped to continue.

He unscrewed the bottle and poured it onto the impromptu pedestal. It darkened as it sagged and threatened to collapse so he poured the second half on the piles of paper on the floor around it before throwing the rest into the corner.

"Your move", again.

No response.

Mark pulled out a match from his back pocket and walked to the bottom of the stairs. He surveyed the room, looking for a disturbance or a crack in the wall that could be hiding the fear of an opponent.

"Your move"

Analysing every shadow like the pieces on a chess board, he looked for a response. For something to come in and break the check he'd put them in.

"Zugzwang"

Mark lit the match and flicked it. It landed at the base of the cardboard plinth and the tiny spark sent a shockwave of fire through the room. Mark was taken aback by how unexpected the growth was, expecting the burn to at least spread at a visible pace but within a second any visible trace of Paula had been swallowed by the risen wall of orange flame. Mark watched for that second, hypnotised by the flames as they danced gleefully over the room. Mark hopped back to step away from the heat and onto the bottom step.

Mark turned to get out but when he took his second step up the stairs he heard an almighty noise.

Before he could react the orange light was replaced. A column of blue fire erupted from the corner of the room and crashed into the ceiling, spilling out over the roof of the basement and turning the beams holding the house up into a sky of fire. Mark fell backwards and caught himself on a metal shelf before he could stumble and bash his head on his spirit fridge. The vibrant mixes of orange and blue fire would be hypnotic if not for the volatile movements they made where they intersected. Like a stormy sea falling upwards rather than down, they waved and crashed together as the blue continued to lunge towards him.

Mark panicked and looked around for a way out. The burning sea of flame had leaked its way through the door and into his home already as his fire alarm finally began to kick into life, he knew that his home was already becoming an inferno and that he needed to get out a faster way than that.

As another burst of blue erupted from the corner, this time more intentionally angled towards him he climbed onto the fridge and pressed himself into the opposite corner.

Since the door was inaccessible he looked at the window, it was slightly lower than the top of the wall so he knew he could get through it only skimming through the flame. Mark looked again at the still burning masses. The column of orange was starting to dwindle and was being overtaken by the colder, hotter flames that began creeping towards his corner.

Keeping as low as he could, he ran his hand across the wall until he felt the bottom of the frame, quickly gripping onto the grooves. The plastic was burning hot but he closed his eyes and immediately leant over and grabbed with his other hand, pulling as hard as he could. He screamed in pain as he did but overclocked every muscle as he desperately pulled himself across and up into the gap.

Another explosion behind him, this time a brilliant white that blinded him through his closed eyelids. He reached into his garden and grasped onto a mass of ground firm enough to anchor him and pulled again. Getting the last of him through he scrambled backwards and onto the damp grass. Pressing his hands into the dirt desperately trying to dull the burning, the whole time trying to kick off his jeans that had themselves been lit by the final conflagration.

He finally finished screaming as he ran out of breath and collapsed in the grass. Looking down himself to his home which was now engulfed in fire, fire he thankfully thought was orange. The blue flames still visible through the window into the basement quickly died out and were replaced with regular flame. The fire stopped ebbing towards him and returned to its natural state of spreading to anything. He watched through the back windows as it entered his kitchen, his bathroom, his spare room. He couldn't see his bedroom from this side of the house and was forced to imagine that.

The thought of his desk, his laptop, his bed, his failed manuscripts and whatever he'd forgotten to pick up of Paula being turned to ash were the last things he thought of before he felt all the thoughts in his head flush away into the black of the sky. Not even the stars piercing through.

XVII

The first thing Mark saw the next time he was conscious was his own name. The proper name: MATTHEW MOSYNE BISHOP, in a clinical black text. He could barely muster up the energy to keep his eyes open for more than a few seconds, let alone move his neck, so couldn't immediately gather why it was written so matter-of-factly. He tried to focus on finding a reason why it was written but got stuck trying to think any further than his own name.

He tried listening instead, he focused on a distinct clicking sounds he could heard. A rhythmic mechanical clicking that interrupted the near-zen silence that surrounded it. The clicking was almost attached to him. He held his breath in anticipation and doing so stopped the clicking. It was a breathing machine. He continued this way, starting with only his observations and painting himself a mental picture of where he was.

Mark was in a hospital bed. He let out a wheeze that was masquerading as a sigh of relief and made himself open his eyes again. Back onto his name he looked around, it was a clipboard left on the bedside table. He rolled his eyes around and saw the right mixtures of greens and whites to confirm where he was. He turned his head and saw a nurse standing around checking on a neighboring bed. Mark wheezed again and caught his attention, giving a nod and letting him know that he was awake. Mark then closed his eyes again. This time in comfort knowing that he had definitely escaped whatever mess he was in. Mark let himself rest.

Mark was eventually woken up from his rest by a nurse coming in and taking away the clipboard. He opened his eyes again and focused in the nurse who noticed Mark waking up and gave a businesslike but ultimately comforting smile. The nurse quickly inspected him to gauge a reaction.

"Good afternoon Mr.Bishop. Good to see you're doing better." He picked up my data and skimmed it. "Good timing, you've just had a visitor and I came to see if you were in a state to give them permission to come in"

I bemusedly took the information as I processed it at half the rate I usually would. "Who is it?"

"Just said she was a friend. Shall I go down and ask?"

"No, no just send her up."

"Good good, she can't stay long though, burn specialist is said they'd want to see you when you're awake again"

"Uh… sure." Mark was confused by such a simple request. Having to consciously conclude why after climbing out of a burning building he might be in need of some burns treatment. He looked down at his hands and winced at the sight of both being buried in a ball of bandage. He tried to move his fingers but struggled to receive any understandable feedback from them. He tried the rest of his body. Kicking off a bit of the bottom of his sheets he got a look at his feet. Both were in far lighter bandages, he could wiggle both sets of toes and on one foot he could feel the feedback of the cloth pressing against him as he did. Looking into the reflections of the bedframe he couldn't make out any facial scars in the warped image and was at least thankful for that.

While looking at his own reflection he could see someone approach from the end of the room and instantly recognised who it was. It wasn't what he looked like that tipped him off, even in the warped reflection he could feel that tingle in the pit of his stomach growing as he thought who was sitting down next to him.

Mark put on a brave face "Hello Polly".

Mark felt like everything he looked at was still out of focus but through that he still saw the same glow he saw at Polly the last time he saw her, before anything involving Paula, or Alex, or Ella.

Instead of responding, she reached over and hugged him. As she did he could feel her wrapping around areas that stung to the touch and he nearly let out a whimper of pain but he held it in in an attempt to not look as bad as he did. She pulled back and looked at him, visibly showing how unsure she was as she thought of what to say.

"Mark... what the hell have you been doing to yourself?"

Mark looked away, not sure how to answer.

"I've heard nothing but horror stories from Jason about you for nearly a fortnight now. How did this happen to you?"

"Don't know, guess I've been a mess recently"

She got angry at him for that and he recoiled away before she recomposed herself.

"No, Jason's a mess because he'll not brush his teeth because he forgot where he left his toothbrush. Disappearing for days? Not working? Not responding to dozens of attempts to contact you? That's not a mess that's something seriously fucked up."

"I said I don't know"

"Oh bullshit. You nearly ended up dead because you let your life go to shit. Now's not the time to be all wishy washy about it."

Mark's eyes began to water as he debated how else he could explain his situation. "I don't know means I don't know why. I knew what I was doing was bad, but sometimes things happen you can't explain"

Polly looked at him again, parsing his response with the efficiency of a machine before sighing. "I don't get it. But I don't think I want to." She backed up in her chair and took another look at him.

"I wanted to check up on you sooner but I've been in London the whole time. I spent most evenings worrying about you, Jason was probably sick of me constantly pestering him for updates on you but he knew the most and he still seemed to know nothing, just that you were acting strange."

Mark thought about the last time he responded to a message. He couldn't remember so it had to have been over a week before he started the fire that he'd even checked if anyone had tried.

"You're lucky that piece of shit burnt your house down. Forced you out of that cycle of shutting yourself in."

"What?"

"They reckon the fire was caused by some faulty kitchen appliances you have, or had. The landlord confessed you'd tried to contact him about them and ignored them so they're probably prosecuting him. How have you not heard this yet?"

"No I've only been awake for like an hour, you're the first person I've spoken to" Mark paused and carefully considered what he'd say. "Sounds plausible"

"Well you don't have to worry about it. You'll probably be asked at some point."

That trail ended there and Mark was left to consider how much he'd confess. His landlord was neglectful and he'd suspected for a long time that he was probably in need of intervention but he knew that he himself had to carry a lot of the blame. He knew he'd have to cross that bridge as it came.

The pause was only for a minute but he took that time to look at Polly. He looked at her and saw how shaken she was by what happened. A look of genuine worry that managed to be the first cloud of uncertainty he'd ever seen in her. She was pale, her hair was in a glum mess, her eyes were slightly bloodshot and her actions were stressed. He was finally capable of seeing her as real flesh-and-blood human with problems. Problem that he knew how to ignore even though they were there. Listening to the clicking of the machine he saw how uncomfortable she was, in spite of the fact that she displayed no signs of wanting to leave. He saw Polly, not the image of her.

"How are you feeling, Polly?"

She looked at him, partially shocked that I seemed interested in something so relatively trivial, but partially grateful for a lighter topic.

"I'm okay, my sister had just had a baby and I went to see her."

She loosened up, and Mark smiled. He kept up the smalltalk, constantly asking her questions to keep her talking, and every small detail that she rattled off lightened the mood so slightly.

Mark lost track of time in the chatter and was upset when a Nurse came in halfway through a tangent about her phone running out of battery too fast to let her know to start finishing it up.

"Looks like I have to go, sorry Mark."

"It's all good, where you going now?"

She looked embarrassed "I've got a date this evening, I've got to start getting ready for it."

Mark laughed, finally able to do a proper one under the breathing mask. "Is this the guy I heard you talk about at the party? A different Mark?"

"Yeah, he's really cool."

Mark looked at her squirming about the questions with a schoolgirl's smile, for a brief moment he saw the same glow come back to her. In that moment Mark figured it out.

"I'm happy for you, Polly"

"Thanks, I'll hear from you soon okay?"

Mark tried to give a thumbs up but quickly realised his lack of visible fingers but knew she got the message anyway.

And in an instant he was alone again. Left to his own devices and the clicking of the machine while waiting for someone else to come to him.

Mark thought. He thought about his now burnt down home and what he planned on doing about it. He thought about his job and if he'd have the guts to ask if he could still work there. He thought about seeing Jason again and thanking him being such a good friend through the years. He thought about paying Hayley back for the free breakfast and apologising for being so impersonal to her. He thought about his mum and how he'd want to start repairing that burnt bridge. And above all he thought about how he probably shouldn't have left his phone in his bedroom.

XVIII

Dear Paula.

I don't know why what happened happened. Or why I did what I did. Or why anything to be honest. I don't know what exactly you are. You've spent all the time I can remember in the recent giving me every emotion I've wanted. I've hated all of it. Yet through the whole thing it never felt like you were trying to teach me a lesson because every time I'd look there was nothing to find. I think I know one more thing now though. In my whole time looking for a you I never tried thinking of your reason why. So whether you're some spirit that came to teach me a lesson or you're a forlorn spawn of my own madness that maybe didn't even exist the whole time. Maybe you're something else. I don't care. I now know what I need to know. So I feel like I can finally let you go.

Mark.

27216923R00070

Printed in Great Britain
by Amazon